INTIMATE MERGERS

RALEIGH DAVIS

The lawyers lined up in front of me are about to shit their pants.

I fold my hands on my desk—polished teak with carved legs, an heirloom acquired by my great-grandfather—and savor the sight. Six of them in crisp wool suits, sweating through their imported linen shirts.

I'd enjoy it more if my day were going slightly better and if the legal eagles in my office could give me what I want. It's one thing to twist the knife if it means getting your way. It's less fun if you can't.

"Are you seriously telling me you can't get anywhere with this case?" I keep my question cold and focused with no hint of anger. Abusing your underlings is for uncultured people, new-money families. And as my mother is so fond of reminding me, we're definitely not that.

A ripple goes through them. That's what they've been saying for the past ten minutes, lined up like guilty schoolchildren. Normally I'd meet with them in the conference room, offer them all a seat and refreshments, but I knew going into this meeting I wasn't going to be happy. So I made sure there were plenty of subtle and not-so-subtle indications that I expected more from them.

The lead lawyer, a man in his early fifties, clinging as he would to a lifeline to the last wisps of hair circling his skull, clears his throat. He's argued before the Supreme Court, but I'm not impressed. "I've never seen anything like this. All my contacts at Immigration Services, the second they hear her name, they hang up. Nobody there wants to even touch this case."

Grace Li. That's her name, the one nobody at USCIS wants to hear. They don't want to speak about her; they just want to deport her.

This dream team of lawyers was supposed to stop that. And now they're telling me they can't do a damn thing.

I want to pinch the bridge of my nose, to massage away the building pressure there, but I won't give away any weakness. I've been trained since birth to never give anything away. "I can't believe no one will talk to you. Isn't this America? What happened to due process of law?"

"Technically, noncitizens aren't entitled to that. And Corvus wants her gone. Like yesterday."

I don't need this lawyer to tell me one of the biggest tech companies in Silicon Valley wants Grace gone. They've been fighting to get her deported from the second they fired her. Without the H-1B visa sponsored by Corvus, Grace can't stay in the country.

Or at least if it weren't for my efforts and these lawyers I've spent a fortune on. This is what I do—the kind of problem I usually solve with a wave of my hand. In addition to the lawyers, I've gotten her job offers, positions with some of the most respected companies in tech, companies more than willing to take responsibility for her H-1B, but Immigration has said no to all of it.

It's not hard to figure out who's whispering in their ear. Corvus is one of the biggest contractors for the NSA, CIA, *and* the Department of Homeland Security. No matter how good my lawyers are, they won't have contacts like the ones

Corvus does in Immigration. Hell, Corvus has tentacles twined around them, not just contacts. Which means they can make Immigration dance to their tune.

No matter how much money and legal talent I throw at this problem, Grace will be deported.

I shouldn't be so upset. This was never meant to be my problem, only a simple favor I was doing. It's not some deep, personal failure.

Still, I can't give up. I can't explain why—perhaps it's because I almost always get my way and have since I was a boy—but I'm not admitting defeat. And neither are these lawyers. Not yet.

I press my palms into my desk. "There must be something more we can do. She's got an interview at Pixio today—she's definitely got the job." I talked to Jack, the CEO, this morning on his personal cell. He assured me it would be fast-tracked, and we arranged to meet up for some polo this weekend. He's convinced Golden Gate Park to reopen the field there for actual polo just for him. And I played a fair amount in college and high school, although I have to borrow horses here. "They won't even be impressed by Pixio?"

All the lawyers exchange a glance. A glance that says *I don't want to be the one to deliver the bad news.*

The head lawyer—Wickersham is his name—is the one to throw himself on the grenade. He clears his throat again, which irritates me so much I'm almost tempted to tell him to knock it off. "I don't think they'll be satisfied by anything. There's nothing that's going to move them on this." He swallows hard. "I'm so sorry."

He doesn't need to make it sound like he's giving a cancer diagnosis. Like I said, this wasn't supposed to be my problem.

It's a friend-of-a-friend thing, which given my network of contacts, happens a lot. Grace worked for Corvus. She'd shared an apartment with her best friend, January, until

Grace had moved into Corvus housing, essentially disappeared, and discovered Corvus had illegal spyware installed on pretty much everyone's phone.

January found out when she was searching for Grace's whereabouts, about the same time she hooked up with Mark —okay, they actually fell in love, but that's the boring part of the story—and Mark is one of my best friends and another partner at Bastard Capital. They rescued Grace from Corvus, stopped the spyware, and now January and Mark are going to live happily ever after. The end.

But there's no fairy-tale ending for Grace. She was fired. Which put her visa in jeopardy.

That's where I come in. Since Mark is my friend and I know everyone—and I mean everyone—I offered to help with Grace's situation. Across all six continents, I know anyone who's worth knowing, the powers both in front of and behind the curtain. And if I don't know them, I know someone who does. I'm two degrees of separation away from anyone who matters.

Of course, if we were talking about Antarctica, you'd be shit out of luck. Although I could probably pull some strings there too, given enough time.

Apparently I'm shit out of luck with American Immigration though.

The plan was to get Grace a new job, transfer sponsorship of her H-1B visa, and she'd be home free. Well, except for that huge conspiracy she uncovered at Corvus. But Grace is a smart woman; she knows to keep her mouth shut. All the information she sent to January about the program was shared anonymously, and she hasn't uttered another peep, publicly or privately.

It doesn't matter though. Corvus is determined to ship her back to China no matter what. Probably as punishment for that conspiracy she uncovered.

I don't know what I'm going to tell Mark. Mark would do

anything for January. January would do anything for Grace. And I'm going to help Mark any way I can, so here we are. With me reaming out these useless lawyers and Grace off at a job interview that will get her nowhere.

Once I'm done with these guys, I'm pouring myself a nice stiff drink. Just the one, because any more wouldn't be classy. But damn do I need it.

I pitch my voice low, making them work to hear me. "There has to be something else. I thought you were the best immigration lawyers in the world."

They are, because they got Archie Chu out of his little… *incident* a few years back. Archie crashed his Ferrari on the 280 one evening, going way too fast with way too much alcohol in his system. The fire was so bad the freeway was shut down for the entire day, and when the cops booked him, it turned out his visa wasn't exactly valid.

He called me in a panic, asking for help. His cousin was school friends with my sister, which meant that I was obligated to help. So I hired Wickersham here, and he started calling people at USCIS, and Archie's situation was all cleared up in a few weeks.

The lawyers flinch at my words. Because of course they consider themselves the best—look at what they charge hourly—but the fact they can't make any headway on this clearly galls them.

I'm trying very hard not to imagine Grace's face when I tell her this news. Her bright, inquisitive eyes will dim, her lush mouth will twist, and her striking cheeks will go white. Her chest might start to rise and fall as she holds in her tears—

This is exactly what I'm not supposed to be thinking about. She's a friend of a friend. She can't be anything more, not even in my fantasies. It's not fair to her. She's vulnerable and depending on me. And I've failed her.

"This is a very… *unusual* case." One of the younger

members of the team, a woman, says that. She doesn't look quite as abashed as all the rest. "The order for her to leave comes from the very top. Unless you have the ear of the president himself, there's not much more to be done."

I do have a backdoor connection to the president, which I've already tapped to help me here, but sadly my connections aren't as powerful as Corvus's.

It's over. I know it is, but I don't let that show in my expression. "I don't want to hear that," I say. "What I want to hear is that you're working on new angles. Constantly. We're not giving up on this until the moment she's actually loaded onto a plane."

That moment is going to be in less than sixty days, the amount of time an H-1B visa holder can stay once they lose their job. But I'm not ready to admit that to the lawyers. Although I'll have to admit it to Grace so she can prepare for the worst.

Damn.

The lawyers continue to hover, some of them looking eagerly toward the door. I suppose they're not used to getting their asses chewed out for failure. They're waiting for my dismissal, knowing I'm too powerful a client to leave without my explicit say-so. I let them sweat a few seconds longer, just to remind them who's paying their exorbitant bills. Not that it will make a dent in my fortune, or even a scuff, but you don't get wealthy and stay there for several generations by wasting money.

"I want something better than this and soon." I nod toward the door. "The clock is ticking."

If any of them wonder why I'm so worked up about a random nobody and her visa, they don't let on. Instead, they file out with obvious relief.

It's not fair of me to call Grace a random nobody, although that's what my mother would do.

My mother's more of a snob than I am, but she wouldn't

be wrong about Grace, at least not at first glance. There are millions of tech workers like Grace in Silicon Valley, all of them holding an H-1B visa and hoping if they can keep their jobs for five years, they'll earn their green cards.

I couldn't help but get to know Grace better as we worked on her case, and those first impressions were wrong. She's driven but also compassionate. She wants to stay and she wants to expose her ex-employer's wrongdoing, but she doesn't want anyone she left behind at Corvus to get hurt because of her actions. I don't let myself think of her much beyond that. I can't help but think about how attractive she is, which is more than enough trouble for me.

I get up and head over to the bar in my office, which sits against one wall. All the partners have them—me, Mark, Logan, Finn, Elliott, and Dev—but I usually only use mine when I have company. Drinking alone isn't my style, but today I need it. Because Grace is going to walk in my office in about an hour, relieved and hopeful and excited about her new job prospect, and I'll have to kill the light in her eyes stone dead.

Disappointing people is part of my job. I have to tell people no all the time: no, I won't be funding their proposal; no, their great idea isn't so great; no, there's no way to save their company. I'm pretty good at being diplomatic but firm. Which is what I'll have to be with Grace.

Grace…

I grab a glass and shake my head. I tell myself this is going to be like any of the million times I've had to say no, but I was never good at lying to myself. It *will* be different, but I'm going to have to pretend it isn't. If I'm calm and keep my polite smile in place, Grace will take this much better than if I'm angry or frustrated. Even though I'm really fucking angry and really fucking frustrated.

Three fingers of single malt ought to do the trick. The

glass is heavy in my palm, and the whiskey smells like heaven if it were filtered through peat.

I stare at our atrium as I sip. All our offices face the atrium, creating a hexagram of glass. Dev's office is directly across from mine, but he's not in there. I can tell because he closes the curtains when he is. Dev's always been the mysterious one, but he's been doing that more and more lately. Closing himself off even further from the rest of us. I'd ask him what's up, but he'd never answer.

Speaking of what might be up with Dev, our office manager, Anjie, steps into the atrium. She gives me a wave and a smile, and I raise my glass. Anjie's the one who turned the atrium into an orchid's paradise. There are trees and moss and hidden hollow places, all to give the orchids the very best environment to bloom in. Anjie's in there every few hours, checking on her beloved blooms. Grace often can't tear her eyes away from them when she meets with me here.

I take another healthy swallow and prepare my speech to Grace in my head. It's a little trick of mine, to always rehearse before any social situation. When you're at ease, it puts other people at ease. Even if that ease is practiced.

We've done everything we could. That's technically true and an okay way to start, but my mouth twists bitterly as I think about it.

I have contacts in the best tech firms in China. You can find an even better job there. That is definitely true. I can even set her up with enough money to start her own firm in China. She could be her own boss, live close to her family, and never have to worry about immigration bullshit ever again.

She didn't tell me the reason she wants to stay so badly, and I didn't pry. But I know that if it were as easy as her finding a good job there, she wouldn't be fighting so hard to remain here.

Know anyone who's up for a green card marriage? That won't even work anymore—people have tried that trick one too many times. I don't spend even half a second lingering on how my gut twists at the thought of Grace marrying someone else.

I don't want to marry her—I hardly even know her. It's just simple possessiveness. I'm attracted to her, and I can't have her. So my body is reacting primitively.

By the time I get to the last finger of whiskey, I've got something decent worked out. It's not perfect, but it'll do.

My private cell phone rings, the line that only my personal assistant and certain family members and friends have access to. Most likely it's my assistant, but if she's calling, something's up.

Great. Because this day wasn't already shitty enough.

I set down my glass and grab the phone. The caller ID says it's Avery, my assistant. "Yes?"

She doesn't waste a second on niceties, which I appreciate. "I have urgent news from your sister."

My heart rate picks up, just slightly. My sister is vivacious, almost flighty, but she wouldn't call Avery unless it was important. "What?" My assistant is one of the few people I can be blunt with, so I take full advantage.

"Your mother just landed at SFO." My assistant pauses too long, which means I'm going to hate what comes out of her mouth next. "Your sister said that Amelia's with her."

I pick up the glass and quickly drain it. If Mother's dragging Amelia all the way here, that can only mean one thing.

Mother hasn't just brought Amelia—she's also brought an engagement ring. I'm certain of that.

I'm the eldest and the only son—of course I'm going to inherit control of the family assets. Lately my mother's been hinting that it's time for me to come home and assume my rightful place as the head of the family. My father passed when I was young, and my mother's been doing more than fine on her own running things, but it's time for me to step up now.

And get married to a suitable girl. There have been some not-so-subtle hints about that.

Mother seems to have moved on from subtle to pointed, bringing Amelia here. My mother has always thought Amelia would be the perfect bride for me, and Mother's clearly decided to take matters into her own hands.

Just when I thought my day couldn't get any worse.

CHAPTER TWO

I haven't let myself feel this hopeful in a long time.

My feet are practically bouncing off the pavement as I walk to the bus stop on Pixio's main campus. It's filled with trees and flowers and happy, busy engineers on their way to whatever happy, busy thing they're working on. I'm already imagining myself among them, as brightly content as they are.

My imaginings are going to happen, which is why I'm practically floating. The interviewers offered me a job right on the spot, told me they'd arrange everything with Immigration and that they're really looking forward to my starting there.

I've heard that before from the other tech companies Paul's gotten me interviews at. The first time it happened, I let myself hope just like this. Then Immigration said no, they weren't going to transfer sponsorship of my visa to the new company.

I was crushed, but I kept going. On to interviews two, three, four, five, and six, all of them saying yes, they'd love to hire me. And Immigration saying no to all of them.

My hope was completely gone by interview and rejection number three, although I kept going. Going on even when there's no hope is my biggest strength. Or my biggest weakness—I'm not sure which.

This time though, this time I really believe it will happen. Perhaps because Pixio is the biggest company I've gotten an offer from yet—the biggest in the world actually, and there's no way Immigration can say no to them. And perhaps because Paul is having another meeting with the immigration lawyers today. I couldn't make it because of the interview, and they couldn't reschedule. Okay, they haven't had good news for me yet, but if it was bad, they'd have made sure I was there. And if it's good, they'll tell Paul. Even if it's only neutral, that will still be a relief.

I can't explain it, but it feels like events are finally going my way.

Of course, I never would have made it this far without Paul's help. I'm not quite sure how I ended up as his pet project, and I'm trying very hard not to let his attention turn my head. I know his concern is impersonal, that he's only helping me because Mark and January asked him to, but I can't help the flutter of my heart every time I see him. He's got the looks and presence of a great prince from an ancient saga, bold and determined as he leads a massive army against the invaders.

Normally I wouldn't be this silly over a man, but I guess what I've been through the past few months has turned me inside out. And if I'm going to get giddy over someone, Paul is a good choice. With his striking cheekbones, plush lips, and intensely dark eyes to swoon about. Not to mention just how perfectly *nice* he is. How perfectly princely.

I walk right past the bus stop, heading toward the main road. I want to tell everyone the good news in person, and Paul is the person currently closest to me. Bastard Capital is about a twenty-minute walk from Pixio, and while the bus would technically get me there faster, I want to enjoy the sun on my face and the wind in my hair. My father says that a good long walk is one of the best ways to feel alive, and my father never gives bad advice.

He was the one who told me I should go to America and stay there. I've achieved the first part, and I'm doing my best to achieve the second. Family is everything to my father, which is why I took his advice so seriously. It wasn't easy for him to tell me to do this, and I don't want to let him down.

Thanks to Pixio, I won't.

When I first arrived in the States, I thought everything would be perfect, that my life was on track. I finally had my H-1B and was about to work at one of the most exciting companies in Silicon Valley—Corvus Technologies. They were on the leading edge of intelligence and surveillance work and featured in the *Disrupt Dispatch* nearly every day.

Okay, the surveillance stuff gave me pause, but I figured I'd be helping catch criminals. A company like that would never spy on ordinary people. And I didn't have much of a choice—Corvus was willing to sponsor my visa. It was my chance to make my parents proud.

At first everything was golden. I found some great room-mates and became good friends with January. Corvus was… not exactly welcoming, but I was getting along well enough. I could see the next five years going just like that.

And then it all went wrong. Corvus put me on a new secret project, insisted that I move into the company hous-ing, only use the company issued phone, and also limit all my personal interactions. Basically, my entire waking life would be owned by them.

It broke my heart to leave January and cut off contact— and it terrified me that Corvus demanded it—but I couldn't say no because I needed that visa. And Corvus knew it too.

When I found out the real goal of the project was to ille-gally put spyware on everyone's phones, I panicked, of course. I envisioned going to prison for a long, long time simply for working on the software. And not only was it illegal, it was *wrong*. This wasn't supposed to happen here. I came to America to get away from this, and here I was, making it happen.

If my father knew what I was doing, considering what happened to his uncle, he would be horrified. But I couldn't leave the company, and I couldn't tell anyone what I was doing. I also couldn't sit back and do nothing.

So I sent some of the project information anonymously to January.

It was mostly an act of desperation. I had to tell someone, but I couldn't expose myself. January would know I was the one who sent the files, but I'd be able to deny everything if it became public.

What January would do with the information didn't really occur to me. I should have thought about it, but I was in too much of a panic. I had to do something so I could live with myself, but quitting my job and blowing the whistle weren't options.

It all blew up in my face anyway. January designed a system to block Corvus's spyware and then confronted the CEO himself, Arne Fuchs. When that happened, I was fired and tossed out of the building like so much trash.

Of course, there's more to the story—there always is—but those are all the important parts. I'm grateful to January for rescuing me and stopping the spyware. But I'm also a tiny bit pissed at her because I'm about to lose my visa. I probably couldn't have handled five years of Corvus, not with what I was working on, but...

I shut my eyes tight for a moment. This isn't what I want to be thinking about right now. Hopefulness is so rare for me, I want to hold on to it as tightly as I can, not obsess over the past.

When I open my eyes, my mood is back to where it should be. Yes, my firing was awful, but things are getting fixed. It will all be fine.

My phone rings as I come to an intersection. Cars whiz past and exhaust blasts my face, but I don't mind. I'm too happy to let it bring me down.

I fish my phone out of my purse and smile when I see who's calling. January is going to be so excited to hear that I finally got this job. I want to tell her in person, but a phone call will work too. We can go out and celebrate the end of all my legal troubles.

"Hey!" I say. "I was just about to call you. Are you at Mark's office?"

If she's already at Bastard Capital, then we can celebrate together. It'll be perfect.

"No." January's tone isn't as excited as mine. It isn't excited at all. "I just saw the lawyers leave. I grabbed one of them and talked to her before she left."

My feet slow as my heart races, and my palms go clammy. No. They don't know about the Pixio offer yet. Whatever is happening, my news changes all of it. "What did they say?"

January draws in a long breath. "It's not good. No matter what they try, USCIS just won't budge."

That's not anything new. Immigration hasn't budged on my case before. "But I got the job at Pixio. They told me everything would be taken care of." I try to put some brightness in my voice, but it jumps past that into panic.

"The lawyers already know about that," January says sadly.

Which tells me that Paul got me the job. I kind of suspected that, but I tried to put it out of my mind so I wouldn't flub the interview. I'm a great coder and engineer, and I wanted Pixio to know that. I didn't want a pity position.

My mouth opens, air rushing in as I try to breathe past the lump in my throat. Oh God, I'm not getting any position now.

"USCIS basically told them that the order for you to leave

comes from the very top," January says. I hear tears in her tone. "That nothing will be acceptable for your visa sponsorship."

The hope I've had—that stupid, reckless, useless hope—is now completely gone, having popped like a balloon attacked by a tiger. I knew Corvus wasn't going to let me stay. I just knew it, and still I let myself believe. What an idiot I was.

I want to sink down to the sidewalk and howl, but there's no way I'm giving in to that weakness. My parents would die if they knew their daughter was crying on a sidewalk in America somewhere. After everything they sacrificed to get me here, I couldn't embarrass them like that even if they can't see me.

"Are they sure?" I'm pleased with how steady my voice is. It almost sounds like the news didn't affect me at all.

"Yeah. I asked them over and over again, but they insisted." January's voice is cracking. "This is all my fault. Maybe I shouldn't have done anything with the files you sent me."

"Of course you should've," I say automatically. "What they were doing was wrong and illegal."

Except Corvus hasn't really been punished for what they did. The program is shut down, but no one's going to prison. The general public still has no idea the spyware was ever on their phones. I'm the one who pointed out their wrongdoing, and I'm the only one who's going to be punished.

The lawyers are being paid to fight for me, and now they're giving up. How am I supposed to keep fighting on my own? If USCIS rejects the Pixio offer…

They will. I suddenly know that they will, the same way I know gravity exists.

The lawyers know it too, and they don't want to waste their time anymore. Maybe Paul should stop wasting his time too.

God, Paul already knows all about what the lawyers said. He'll have to tell me, and I'll have to pretend to be brave and stoic and meet my fate with my head held high. Right now that scenario seems worse than telling my parents. Paul's been so kind, so helpful, and he didn't even have to be. And I feel like I've just ruined it all.

Of course it isn't my fault—it's all Corvus's fault—but that doesn't make the stone of guilt in my chest any smaller.

"I'm on my way to the office," I tell January. "I'll be there in about fifteen minutes. We can talk more then."

She's sniffling into the phone, which makes my own eyes sting. I blink the tears away because I can't lose it on a public street. That will have to wait until I'm at home.

I'm currently staying rent-free in an apartment that Paul owns. I didn't know he owned the building when I first moved in; I thought the owner was someone who owed Mark a favor. But after talking to the tenants, I realized exactly who my new landlord was. Well, it's really a holding company that owns the building, but a quick Google search showed that it was part of Paul's family holdings and that the same company owns a ton of real estate throughout the Bay Area.

I'm sure it was nothing to Paul to offer me one of the thousands of apartments he owns, but after being kicked out of Corvus with only the clothes on my back, it meant the world to me.

I suppose I'll have to move back in with my parents once I'm home. I'll be glad to see them again, to be close to them again, but they won't be able to hide their disappointment. And I won't be able to prevent being hurt by it.

"I'd love that, but Mark and I have to go," January says sadly. "We have this fund-raiser thing in the City, and we can't miss it. But I'll stop by tonight. I'll bring takeout."

I want just January to come and not Mark, but I can't think of a way to say that without being terribly rude. Commiserating with January sounds lovely, but to have Mark hovering over us, reminding me of how perfect

January's life is turning out, would be too painful. He's a nice guy—scratch that, he's not nice at all, but he adores January —but I just can't handle it.

"Don't worry about me. I think I'm going to call the lawyers myself, see if there's anything more I can do. Maybe…"

I can't even finish that. Defeat has settled over me so hard I can't breathe. But I have to. I have to keep moving forward, toward the office and her and Paul.

"No, I can't leave you alone," she insists.

I won't be alone. I'll have Paul. I don't know where that thought came from. He's never once met me outside his office. Everything about him has been distant, polite, and professional.

Which is probably why I'm so fascinated by him. I've always wanted to touch whatever was just out of reach, and I never lost that urge even when I grew up.

"Honestly, I'll be fine. I'm going to need some time…" I swallow the sob that tries to climb up my throat. "I'm going to need a little bit of time to process this."

January sniffles, and I can hear her wiping her nose. "You're taking this so much better than I am. Not that I'm giving up."

"I'm not giving up either." That's a lie. Already I can feel the fight slipping out of me. The impossibility of all this is suddenly, sharply real to me. Who did I think I was, going up against Corvus? Even with power of the Bastards behind me, I'm no match for them. "But I think it's time for me to be realistic too."

There's some rustling on the other end of the line, and I hear Mark's deep tones although I can't make out what he's saying.

"We have to go," January says. "I'll call you later."

"Sure. Have fun."

I slide my phone back in my bag and force my feet to

keep moving. I don't know why I'm still heading to Bastard Capital since my big triumph is now a big bust and January won't even be around, but I can't think of anywhere else to go. I don't want to be in the apartment that Paul's given me as some favor to a friend. And I don't want to be around strangers.

My father always said that putting off a difficult thing only ever made it worse. He's right, but it's hard for me to put into practice. If I were a better daughter, I'd be dialing my parents right now. Telling them I've failed and I'm coming home will be the hardest thing I've ever done.

But I'm not, so instead I'll go tell Paul I failed. That he doesn't need to be noble and help me out anymore. I'm clearly a lost cause.

Well, I won't be that melodramatic. I'll be polite, grateful, and distant. The same way he's been with me this entire time. That way we can both part with some dignity.

And then I'll go home and start to pack. I'll call the lawyers and see what else can be done while I do it, because I'm not giving up yet.

But I'm also going to face reality. Finally.

CHAPTER THREE

My mother is a force of nature.

Not in the flashy, she's-a-typhoon kind of way. More in the power-of-eons-passing kind of way. Like the river that carved out the Grand Canyon. Slow, steady, and completely unstoppable.

"What a surprise," I say as my mother steps into my office. She's never gotten the hang of sarcasm, so she'll take the comment literally.

My mother—Lillian Tsai—looks her age, which is sixty-two, but it's a beautiful, well-kept sixty-two. Even when I was a kid, I never saw her without her hair done, her nails painted, and her face made up. When my dad died and she took command of the family holdings, she had to wear a mask of perfection in order to fight off scheming cousins. Over the years, she grew into that mask so well she practically is perfect.

I love my mother, but I'm also a little frightened of her.

My assistant hurries in behind her, holding a tea tray with a steaming pot, several delicacies, and china with my mother's signature pattern. Mother travels with her own place settings. As soon as the tea tray hits the coffee table in my office, Avery hurries out again. She's more than a little frightened of my mother.

"I know your sister already called you." Mother sets her quilted Chanel handbag on a chair. She's carried that bag for twenty years—Mother doesn't buy anything new unless she absolutely needs it. She leaves the flashy purchases to new-money types.

"Actually, she already called my assistant." I kiss her offered cheek. "Where's Amelia?"

"I sent her to the hotel. I needed to speak with you before you proposed."

I sigh, wishing I'd downed the entire bottle of whiskey before she got here. "Did you ever think of asking me if I wanted to marry her? Or if she wants to marry me?"

"Don't be silly. It's high time you took over the family holdings, and you'll need a bride to help you with that. You won't want to deal with all the charitable work and social-izing on your own."

"You can't really be thinking of retiring. You're still sharp as ever."

Mother sinks down into one of the chairs and suddenly looks tired. I can't remember if I've ever seen her this tired before. "Thank you for the kind words, but I... I never wanted to do this my entire life. I only built it up so I could hand it off to you."

That's not exactly true. My father died young, of cancer, and before he passed, he arranged everything so that my mother would inherit control of the family holdings. There was a lot of grumbling about it, and she had to fight hard to keep her position, but my father saw what no one else in the family did: my mother was born to run a massive corpora-tion like ours. She might not have been born into our family, but she was the perfect person to manage the assets that kept all of us going.

She's been saying I should take over ever since I turned

eighteen. I mostly ignored her as I went to university, then to business school, then helped start Bastard Capital. She never really did anything about her insistence that I take over, so I never took her seriously.

Until now. Dragging Amelia all the way here and insisting that I propose is a pretty dramatic step. Which is typical of Mother: when she decides something needs to be done, she doesn't hesitate.

Still, I'm not getting married. And not to Amelia. My mother is stubborn, but she'll listen to reason.

"I'm happy to take over and let you have a rest," I say, "but I can't marry Amelia. Does she know that's why you dragged her here?"

My mother waves her hand, the only sign of irritation she allows herself. "I didn't tell her exactly, but she must suspect. Our families have known each other forever. And of course you have to marry her. There are very few women who can deal with the demands that will be made on your wife. Amelia comes from the right kind of family, wouldn't be marrying you for your wealth, and she knows how to move through our social circle. And you two have been friends forever."

That's all true. Amelia would be the perfect wife for me—if I'd never left Taiwan and followed the exact path my mother thinks I should have. But I didn't and I'm not precisely the man my mother thinks I am. I want more from a marriage than what Mother considers to be the perfect wife.

The friends-forever part also means I can't marry Amelia. Because I know that Amelia loves someone else.

She's desperately in love with someone her family would never approve of and has been for years. She's never had the courage to actually do something about it, and while she's miserable now, she'd be even more miserable married to me.

If I tell my mother that, every single detail will reach

Amelia's mother's ears before the end of the day. Mother would consider it her duty to tell Amelia's mother that her daughter is headed for ruin. So I keep my mouth shut.

"I don't see why I have to be married in order to run the company." I try to think of someone else in our social circle who's unmarried and successfully managing the family assets, as proof of principle, but I can't think of anyone. They were probably all steamrolled by their mothers into marrying Amelia clones.

That's not going to happen to me.

My mother simply stares at me for a long moment. I can't tell if she's disappointed or angry or simply thinking up new tactics. She loves me, yes, she's devoted her entire life to me and my sister and running the companies, but she's never once let me win an argument with her.

"I've been doing this all on my own for decades now," she says quietly. "I know how hard it is. And I don't want you to suffer through what I did."

She couldn't have said anything better designed to pierce my heart. I saw exactly what she struggled through as she fought for my father's legacy for us. She couldn't have remarried—the family would've never allowed that—but maybe having someone by her side, someone *on* her side, might've made all of it easier to bear.

"I won't suffer," I say to her. "I know how hard it was, but because you fought so well, it will be easier for me."

She shakes her head. "Once you're running the companies, you won't have time to search for a bride. And even more gold diggers will come out of the woodwork then."

Time to search for a bride. I hold in my instinctive flinch. I came to America to get a break from all that, from always having to be the perfect eldest son, a credit to his mother and his distinguished family name. Here I could just be Paul. Yes, I was still very, very wealthy, but with the freedom of anonymity. Here I could do whatever I wanted. No one was watching my every move.

I knew I'd have to return home and take up that responsibility someday, but I wasn't expecting it to be so soon.

But my mother's right—she's handled everything for decades. If she wants to stop, I have to honor that. And step up and do my duty.

"All right," I say with a heavy heart. "I'll come home with you, take over the day-to-day operations. You shouldn't have to manage everything if you're ready to retire. But I absolutely cannot marry Amelia. It's not happening."

I don't often tell my mother flat-out no, but in this case, I have to.

Her expression goes stony. "It must happen. I've already drawn up the documents for your succession and had them approved by the board. They wanted to have your cousin Oliver take over. Archie, especially, argued for Oliver over you."

This time I do wince. Oliver's nice enough but not very bright. "Archie's only suggesting him because he knows he can control him. If he's in charge, that side of the family will loot everything that isn't nailed down."

My mother nods sharply. "Exactly. Which is why you have to take over. The board agreed to my succession plan —but only if you are at home and suitably settled."

This is like something out of a K-drama. "*Suitably settled?* You mean married?"

"Yes. You return home, have a beautiful society wedding, and begin producing the next generation. That is *suitably settled.* And that's what they want."

The board never suggested any such thing—that's what *she* wants. Oh, the family will be happy enough to have me as the ideal son heading up everything, but I doubt that was their first demand.

I'm not sure how to call her on it though.

My mother holds up a jewelry box from her purse. "I stopped by Paris last week and picked up the engagement ring. You and Amelia will announce your engagement in three weeks at the gala. It's the perfect way to raise awareness and money for our foundation and excellent press for the family."

Our family foundation sponsors the biggest gala in San Francisco, supposedly to raise money for cancer charity. And we do, donating millions upon millions of dollars to cancer researchers at UCSF. But it's really the perfect opportunity to show off how benevolent and rich we are.

But in a tasteful way.

Mother has a plan that would do a general proud. My throat tightens as I realize that she's not letting go of this, not easily.

When she sets her sight on something, she never lets go. Rivals have always called her ruthless, while I've preferred to think of her as tenacious. I'm beginning to see her rivals' point.

If only I could tell her the truth about Amelia… but not even that might stop her. Mother would think that marrying me, even if she doesn't love me, would be much better for Amelia than pining after someone her family wouldn't accept.

My mother might have a point. Amelia's never held a job in her life. Her family would cut her off without a second thought if she married the man she loves, and I can't imagine Amelia working for a living or keeping house.

That still doesn't mean I'm going to marry her. But I can't see an easy way out of this. Not yet.

Mother puts the jewelry box away, then picks up a cup of tea. She takes a long, satisfied sip. "Really, you should be thanking me. I've taken care of everything for you. And Amelia is quite pretty—poor Geoffrey Lai married Jenny

Chung. Such a big fortune, but those ears…" Mother shudders delicately.

My mother doesn't know it, but right after the wedding, Geoffrey moved back in with his longtime girlfriend—mistress now, I guess—and Jenny is shopping her way through Europe, finally spending the inheritance she was never allowed to touch before. They're happy in their own way, but that's not what I would want out of marriage. I'm not even ready to get married, but I don't want that.

I suppose I want a partner somewhat like my mother described—someone who could handle my life, my family, and the spotlight I'm in. But someone not so rigidly… perfect that I couldn't stand her.

A fluttering of leaves in the atrium catches my attention. From behind a fern, Grace appears. She's looking at a black orchid with a white-and-purple center, her hand hovering over it like she's desperate to touch it but afraid to as well.

Something about her expression, the bleak turn of her mouth, the lines around her eyes, the way she won't let herself touch the flower makes my chest do strange, painful things.

As she catches my eye, a current passes through the air from her to me. Not a greeting or even an acknowledgment, but something deeper. Something that makes my skin crackle.

And then she looks away, her cheeks going pink. But that buzz remains between us.

I don't look away. "I can't marry Amelia," I say slowly, my gaze stuck on Grace. A wisp of an idea floats through my mind, a hint of a solution to my fiancée problem.

It would be crazy, but no crazier than what my mother's suggesting. But there's no time to convince her or let her in on the pretense…

"You keep saying that," Mother says, "but you haven't given me a reason."

No, I can't give her the real reason. But a false one might just work.

I turn to look at my mother. "The reason... The reason is because I'm already engaged." I point to the atrium. "To Grace, actually."

CHAPTER FOUR

Of course Paul would be meeting with his mother when I came in. Of course. Because I can't catch a break.

Anjie took one look at my face when I asked for Paul and pulled me into the atrium. I suppose she meant for me to hide behind some ferns while she went to get me some tea, but I can't help but stare at Paul and the woman with him.

Lillian Tsai is even more impressive and imposing in person than she is in photos. I immediately recognize her from all the articles about her that I've devoured. I knew she was Paul's mother, but seeing her here, in his office, is almost too real.

She's famous, infamous, the kind of woman I don't necessarily want to be but am in awe of. Running a massive family company on her own for decades? Yeah, that takes a spine of steel. Doing it with her grace and poise? That takes immense character.

Neither of them notices me, which I'm grateful for. They seem to be… not arguing, exactly, but it's a tense conversation. Not something they want me to catch them at.

Instead, I study some of the orchids, or pretend to. I suddenly feel small and silly, running here to Paul, expecting to cry on his shoulder. We're distant acquaintances at best, and I would embarrass him if I burst into his office all upset.

I should go. He's busy with family things, and he's done more than enough to help me. I'll go home, wait for January to call, and—

He's motioning me to come in. What the hell is he doing that for?

I go so stiff I can feel the air swirling at the bottom of my lungs. His mother is there; he can't mean to introduce me?

Heat prickles along my skin, my nerves waking back up in a rush. He's gesturing again, his expression going from friendly to stern. He's *ordering* me to come in.

So I lift my hand and point to myself, which is so ridiculous I immediately want to die. Brilliant, Grace. No, he clearly wants that orchid next to you to sprout legs and walk into his office.

Paul's nostrils flare long and slow. He's sighing at me. I can't blame him.

I nod, the gesture curt with embarrassment. Right. I can't avoid it now.

I have to walk through the main office to get to Paul's office since there's no other door through the atrium. It's a short distance, but I still pray for Anjie to appear and whisk me off for tea, thereby saving me.

My terrible, awful luck holds, and she doesn't.

When I walk into the office, I clasp my hands in front of me and make my expression soft. I'm going to be introduced to Lillian Tsai. She won't remember me, but I'll definitely remember this.

Paul is smiling at me like… I don't know what that smile means. It's wider than I'm used to but a little bit sharp at the edges, like he's trying to poke me into realizing something. "And here she is." He sounds like he couldn't wait for me to arrive. "You can finally meet her."

He's addressing that to the both of us—he means his mom

meeting me and me meeting his mom. Which is confusing as heck. I'm so lost—I'm going to need a map *and* GPS to find my way through this.

His mom isn't exactly rude, but I can tell from her expression she is not happy about this. Whatever *this* is.

"Grace, this is my mother." He puts a hand in the small of my back and doesn't exactly push but very firmly guides me over to his mother. His hand is warm and large, and my shirt is very thin. My heart kicks up a notch because he's touching me. "Mother, this is Grace. My fiancée."

Fiancée. That's not the word he meant. He said... *Fiancée.*

Fiancée?

I've probably read too many romance novels, because two seconds after my brain processes the word fiancée, I realize what he's up to.

We're fake engaged.

I want to stare at him, to open my mouth and shout, ask him what the hell he thinks he's doing, but something deep in my brain holds me back. Probably my awareness of his mom watching the two of us with a skeptical turn to the corner of her mouth.

This isn't the time or place to confront him, so instead I blink to clear the cobwebs from my mind, then put on a smile. Small, polite, almost shy. Deferential in the extreme degree.

"I'm so glad to meet you." I bow, just a touch lower and longer than I need to. "I'm sorry I wasn't prepared for your arrival."

I guess I'm playing along here if only because I don't know what else to do.

I know better than to say, *Paul didn't mention you were coming.* That would be casting blame on him, and no one can cast blame on the favored son except for her. At least that's how these things usually go.

She holds out her hand and squeezes my fingers briefly.

Her expression remains impassive. I get the sense she's not angry with me but rather with Paul. But she can't light into him in front of me.

I know the feeling, because the second she leaves, *I'm* going to let Paul have it. I don't care how nice he was about the whole immigration thing, springing a fake engagement on me is *not* cool.

Although this is going to make for a terrific story to tell January. I'm sure I'll laugh about it later, although it's definitely not funny at the moment.

"Paul hasn't told me much about you," she says. "I'm looking forward to getting to know you."

"I wanted you to meet each other before I said anything." Paul says that as smooth as anything, as if he's not lying his ass off right now, right to his mother's face. I'm impressed in spite of myself.

"And now we've met." His mother is just as smooth, if quite a bit cooler. "When were you planning on announcing this? I presume you haven't told your sister yet."

There is the smallest flicker around Paul's eyes. No, his sister has no idea what's going on. I've never met her, but I know she lives around here. And it sounds like I'm about to meet her too. And I'll have to pretend to be madly in love with her brother. Again.

Just an hour ago, I thought everything in my life was settled. And now I'm a few weeks away from being deported *and* I'm fake engaged. As soon as my brain catches up with all this, it's going to explode.

Involuntarily my eyes travel over Paul. It won't be hard to pretend with him, not with his classically handsome appearance. Who wouldn't fall for a man who looks like a fantasy prince?

He suppresses the flicker quickly. "I was going to surprise you both."

"Yes, he thought it would be nice." I could bite my tongue

off once that comes out of my mouth. I don't know why I'm trying to support Paul—he's not the kind of man who springs surprises, and his mother certainly doesn't look like the kind of woman who'd enjoy them.

"Hmm." No, his mother is definitely not into this surprise. She picks up her purse, clearly done with meeting me. "I'm glad Paul finally saw fit to introduce us. We can hear all about your engagement at dinner tonight. Make us reservations at the usual place. I really shouldn't leave Amelia alone any longer."

I don't know who this Amelia is, but the mention of her name makes Paul's mouth tighten. It's not his sister, so who is she?

As his mother leaves, she gives Paul a peck on the cheek. For me she has a nod. I can tell from the inquisitive spark in her eyes that she's going to be furiously Googling me the second she walks through the door. I can't say I blame her.

She shuts the door quietly behind her, the precision of her gesture a sharper rebuke than a slam would've been.

I stare out at the atrium, counting backward from one hundred, listening for the sounds of her footfalls to fade. When there's complete silence, I count backward from one hundred once more and then round on Paul.

"What in the hell?"

He blinks at me. "I didn't know that you swore."

I curl my hands into fists. He's gorgeous and wealthy and charming, but that is just about the dumbest thing he could've said. "Really? Because I didn't know we were *engaged*."

His expression flattens. Oh, the prince is displeased with my rebellious attitude. "It was an extreme situation. If you hadn't been here, I wouldn't have had to involve you."

Of all the excuses… I'd like to throw something at his too-noble profile, but there's nothing close by. "So somehow it's my fault? Wrong place, wrong time?"

He gestures to one of the chairs, silently asking me to sit. I shake my head. I'm too keyed up to restrict myself to a chair. I'd rather start pacing.

But I won't. It would be bad form to start doing that. At least I can stand and wrap my arms around myself and tap my toes in my shoes. I'll allow myself that much agitation.

Paul sighs at my refusal. He starts to cross his arms, then stops himself.

He wants to sit, but he can't until I do. The realization dawns on me when his shoulders slump, exhaustion radiating from him. In spite of what he's just done, I actually feel sorry for him.

So I take one of the chairs, the one nearest to the atrium. The sight of all those orchids and ferns and greenery is soothing, and I definitely need some serenity right now.

Paul takes a chair across from me, leaning in so close that our knees almost brush. "I'm sorry. I wouldn't have sprung something like that on you unless it was necessary."

I fail to see how a fake engagement could ever be necessary, but I soften in spite of myself. It's his eyes, so imploring, dark and bright as polished obsidian, pulling me in no matter how mad I try to stay.

"What happened?" I ask.

"First tell me about the Pixio interview." He's trying to do his usual smile—and failing.

I don't smile back. "I already talked to January after she talked to the lawyers. I know it's all hopeless."

I hate the way my voice breaks on *hopeless*. Hate it more than I've hated anything before. Apparently I can pretend to be engaged, but pretending my fight isn't already lost is beyond me. I'm just so tired of it all. So tired.

Being deported might almost be a relief at this point. At least it would be over.

Paul walks over to the bar against one wall and pours me a stiff drink. When I shake my head at him, he forces it into my hand. "If there was ever a moment to take up drinking, this is it." His smile is almost crooked, a charming one I've never seen before. "And it's not hopeless. Not yet. So, bottom's up."

I take a small sip just to be polite. I know whiskey is supposed to be delicious, and I'm sure Paul has nothing but the best, but I never really developed a taste for it. I like neon-pink drinks with more sugar than alcohol. Which is probably not something I should admit to him.

He nods when he sees me take a drink. "Feeling better?"

I'm not actually. I set the glass down and fix him with a look. "So, why is it so necessary for us to lie to your mother about something as big as an engagement?"

He actually turns pink. Not red or flushed or any of those manly ways to describe embarrassment. No, this is definitely an ashamed you-caught-me-out pink.

He still manages to look wickedly handsome doing it though.

"My mother just arrived today. And she brought a fiancée for me."

My eyebrows shoot up to my forehead. So that's the Amelia his mother left at the hotel then. I'm not against parents having a say in who you marry—maybe even a little bit more than a say—but just showing up at the San Francisco airport with a fiancée? That's a little bit much.

Okay, that's *a lot* much.

I grab the glass and take another sip. It's burn-y and marsh-y and the opposite of what I'd want to put in my mouth. But the one good thing I can say is that it's already going straight to my head.

"You don't want to marry her?" I ask. I doubt his mother picked out someone horribly unsuitable.

"It's not that…" Paul lifts his hands. "I mean, I don't particularly *want* to marry her, but Amelia wouldn't be a *bad* wife. She knows everyone I know, our families are friends, and she'll know how to deal with all the crap I have to put up with."

I don't let myself make a face. She sounds like quite the paragon. She's probably someone who's exactly the right height and exactly the right weight according to the fashion magazines and says and does exactly the right thing all the time.

A pulse of jealousy spears my heart. It's silly, because I'll never be that woman, and I don't particularly want to be, but the way he makes her sound so *perfect*...

"So why can't you marry her again?" It sounds like he doesn't really have any strong feelings about her, good or bad.

"She's in love with someone else. She has been for a long time, except her family would never accept him. Marrying me would make her miserable."

And what about you? Would you be miserable with her? But I don't dare ask. It's clear that if there wasn't this other man in the picture, he'd be perfectly happy to marry this woman to make his mother happy.

I take another sip and shiver as the whiskey travels down my throat. I think that's more than enough of that.

I set the glass back with a firm thump. "So instead you pretended to be engaged to me? Why can't you just tell your mother how Amelia feels?"

He slumps deeper into the chair, his legs spreading wide. The soft fabric of his pants pulls tight against his thighs, lovingly outlining them.

I swallow hard and most definitely do not let my gaze travel any higher up his legs.

"If I tell my mother," he says, "she'll tell Amelia's mother, and then all hell will break loose. Amelia is miserable now, but if her mother finds out, she's going to be somewhere beyond miserable."

So he's going to use me to save the feelings of this other

woman. I know I'm supposed to be grateful to him for helping me, but that hurts. It hurts a whole lot. I don't want to just be a tool for him to use because I was handy.

He can find some other girl to pretend to love him—with his wealth and looks, he could find a million girls. It doesn't have to be me.

I'm halfway tempted to tell him that I don't want to help him, that he needs to find someone else for his little charade, but then I remember everything he's done for me. The lawyers, dealing with USCIS, all the job offers I've gotten, including the one at Pixio: that was all Paul. I never asked him to do any of that—he did it to help me.

And now he's asking me to do this.

Really, it's not that big of a deal. We're not actually going to be married. I pretend to be in love with him—considering how hot he is, it won't be much of a stretch—and then in a few weeks or so I leave at the request of the US government. Oh, Paul's said it's not hopeless, not yet, but it is. There's a definite end date on this.

Of course, I'd be lying to his entire family, but if Paul's okay with it, then I suppose I can be too.

There's just one tiny problem… "I'm not at all the kind of woman your mother would want you to marry."

I'm not ashamed of my background or my family, but it's still worlds away from his. I'm not a *paragon* like Amelia.

Paul sits up, no doubt sensing I'm about to give in. "That's why we're going to make you over. And I'll give you a crash course on everyone in my family while we do."

Oh no. I'm good at exams—you have to be in order to make it through the Chinese education system and then on to America. But this kind of test sounds like absolute hell.

"Your mother won't suspect?" I ask. Because I'm pretty sure she wasn't buying what we were selling earlier.

"Oh, she already suspects." He shrugs. "But this will buy

me enough time to get Amelia back home and figure something out."

That doesn't sound like much of a plan. "Maybe you can find someone else to marry?" I suggest. "Like, for real."

He makes a face. "There's no way in hell I'm getting married right now. My mother wants to retire and have me take over the family holdings, but she's insisting that I need a wife. Someone to help me navigate the social situations, the business deals, the family. All of it."

Paul doesn't agree with that at all, and his expression invites me to see it his way.

But… his mother isn't wrong. I can see her point about him needing someone to lean on as he handles that. It sounds daunting, dealing with business and family and having to do it entirely on your own.

I know too well how fraught family connections can be.

Still, it's his life. I'm not his mother, and I can't force him to marry. His plan is still flawed though. "Once I'm gone, she'll just forget about you getting married?" I ask skeptically.

"I wasn't really thinking it all the way through." He smiles, mostly to himself. "She just showed up, insisted that I needed to propose to Amelia immediately, and then I saw you in the atrium. The plan formed itself."

"You're being way too generous in calling it a plan."

His eyes narrow as he studies me. "Maybe this *will* work out. I'll go home to take charge of the family business, but you'll stay here or…"

I finish it for him because I'm too depressed to dance around it any longer. "Or I'll be deported, you mean."

He doesn't flinch at the word *deported*, which I have to give him credit for. "No, no matter what happens, we're not going to end up in the same country ever. I'm definitely leaving for Taipei, and you *might* be leaving. *Might*."

I nod tiredly. Suddenly I'm just exhausted by it all. By

fighting to stay here, by even considering his proposal, by trying to decide what to do with everything I know about Corvus and their illegal methods. It's all just too much.

I only wanted a normal job, to work my five years, then get my green card. I never wanted to cause trouble. I know all too well what happens to troublemakers. That was never going to be me.

"All right," I say, quiet and dull. "I'll do it."

"Are you sure?" The concern in his voice makes my heart trip. I tell it to knock it off. It's not anything personal on his end. "You can say no. I'll tell my mother… something."

"You can't tell your mother that you lied." I give him a small smile. "I know how well that'll go over."

He reaches over and takes my hand. It's a friendly gesture, and of course we'll have to be even more intimate than this if we're pretending to be engaged, but my body snaps awake anyway. He's never touched me before, and now he's done it twice in several minutes, and this is totally going to fail if I can't keep my reactions under control.

His mouth is open like he wants to say something, but instead he stares at my hand. The one that he's holding.

Then his expression slides back into his usual distant but polite mask. "I promise this won't be as bad as it sounds. We'll have a few family dinners, and…" His jaw tightens. "Oh shit, I forgot all about that."

Whatever *that* is it sounds horrible and torturous. Something I definitely don't want to do.

"What?" I asked warily. I kind of want to pull my hand free of his, and I also kind of don't want to.

Maybe I'll have to go play mah-jongg with his mother and aunts or prepare dinner for them or… or… or….

I can't think of anything worse than that, actually.

Paul drops my hand, steeling his expression. Oh no.

"There's a gala my family puts on every year," he explains. "Well, the foundation my family supports puts it on, with all the proceeds going to the medical research the foundation funds. It's coming up in a month, and my mother was expecting me to announce the engagement to Amelia there."

My nerves are starting to shake because I can see where this is going. All right, there was something worse I hadn't thought of. I wet my lips. His gaze follows my tongue.

"So instead we're going to announce *our* engagement there?" I point between the two of us to emphasize how horrid I find that.

"It's what they're expecting." He at least has the grace to look apologetic. "And this way, you won't have to worry about the press until after the gala."

My cheeks go numb. "The press?" I squeak out.

"You don't have to worry about them," Paul says quickly. "We'll keep the news just in the family for now, make it public at the gala."

Right, because he's famous and in the press a lot. And I will be too, apparently, at least after this party. I run my hand over my face. It's a ball, or rather a *gala*, and if I were Cinderella, it would be perfect. The perfect cap and ending to my fairy tale.

Except I'm not Cinderella. I'm just Grace, unemployed, about to be deported, and mixed up with a man who's way too wealthy for me.

If only a missing shoe was the worst of my problems.

I might have sounded more confident about making over Grace than I actually was.

To be honest, she looks fine to me, perched in one of the chairs in my office. More than fine in a pencil skirt that hugs her hips and thighs and a silky top that clings to her breasts. She's sexy in a prim and proper, buttoned-up way, which drives me crazier than it should.

I need to be thinking about making this deception work, not about how her waist dips in just so, the peep of her bra strap at the edge of her collar, or sliding that skirt up her thighs. None of that stuff should be in my brain. Except I can't shake it loose now.

Shit. This is going to be tougher than I thought.

"Chanel," I say, my brain finally connecting to something more than *Goddamn, Grace looks hot.*

Grace, who's taking all this way better than she should, gives me a look of polite confusion. "Sorry, I don't think there's any Chanel in my closet."

Is she being sarcastic? I'm not quite sure. She's never been sarcastic with me before.

"We'll fix that," I say, picking up the phone. A quick call to my assistant will settle everything.

Once I'm done arranging it, I study Grace. There's not enough time to brief her on the entire family, but we can start with the basics. Thank God she's got a quick brain.

"So, you met my mother."

She nods. "Lillian Tsai."

"You know her?" I ask. She rolled that off faster than I was expecting.

"Yes." She cocks her head. "Don't you know how famous your mom is?"

I know she's famous back home and among the international business community. I didn't think she'd be famous enough to come to Grace's attention. "She's my mother," I say. "I don't really think about it."

"How did we meet?" Grace asks.

"We met when…" I pinch the bridge of my nose. "Shit. I guess our actual meeting isn't going to fly as a romantic encounter."

I was so focused on getting her up to speed on the family I didn't think about what they'd ask us. And the lies we'll have to produce on demand.

"How should we meet?" I ask. "I've never read a romance."

"A man who sneers at romance—how surprising."

Okay, that's definitely sarcasm. And I wasn't *sneering*. "Sorry, we business titans usually choose *The Economist* for some light bedtime reading. No fake engagements there."

Although there have been more than a few political marriages that I've been suspicious about. There's no way the French president's wife is *that* in love with that asshole.

"We met…" She taps her chin. I've never noticed it before, but there's the tiniest cleft there. Hard to see with the eye, but I bet I could totally find it with my tongue.

Settle down, I order my libido.

Grace snaps her fingers, almost making me jump. I need to quit fantasizing about her if I'm going to be able to think fast enough to lie tonight at dinner.

"Mark and January," she says. "It's so simple—we met through Mark and January. Which is true; we'll just have to add some extras. He's your best friend, she's my best friend, and when we met, we just *knew*."

"Knew what?"

Grace stares at me. "Knew we were meant for each other."

Right. That. "Okay, we met through Mark and January, and it was love at first sight. That's easy enough." Now that's settled, we can get down to the family tree.

"How did you propose?"

I blow out an exasperated breath. I forgot about that little detail. That's going to be the first thing Lucy asks me.

"We have to tell my sister," I say. "There's no way I could make her believe this. Her name's Lucy, by the way."

"What will she say?" Grace isn't happy about that idea.

"She'll tease me, threaten to tell our mother, and then take the secret all the way to the grave."

Grace smiles as if she can't quite believe it. I wonder if she has any siblings.

Another detail I'll need to know. "Do you have any brothers or sisters?"

"No. It's just me."

The lingering wistfulness in her tone hits me right in the chest. I want to tell her my sister is mostly a pain in the ass, but I don't.

Before I can say anything, there's a knock at my office door. And then the clerk from Chanel is wheeling in an entire rack of clothes.

Because I don't know the first thing about what Grace should wear tonight, I fell back on my mother's favorite designer for an emergency shopping session.

It's a little bit cliché to dress your fiancée—*fake* fiancée—in your mother's favorite designer in order to impress said mother, but I'm running out of time. So Chanel it is, even though I'm not a particular fan of theirs. Those tweed suits remind me of too many Sundays spent in church or after-noon teas with aunts who loved to squeeze my cheeks and scold me. Also, the tweed suits strike me as kind of ugly.

But I don't tell Grace any of that. She's got to be excited about Chanel, or at least pretend to be, if this is going to work.

When she sees the rack of clothes, Grace's eyes go wide. "That was fast."

The sales clerk smiles ingratiatingly at me. "Anything for Mr. Tsai. Will your mother be visiting us while she's here?"

I have no idea how she already knows my mother is in the City. Maybe from my mother's Instagram feed. Considering how much my mother spends at Chanel, it would be a good move to stalk her on social media.

And yes, my mother has an Instagram account. When my sister showed her she could share pictures of her meals with family and everyone else around the world, my mother became addicted. I think she also enjoys being an influencer, though she'd never admit it.

"Maybe," I say with a polite, distant smile. "I'm not quite sure what she has planned for this trip."

"We always love seeing her." There are dollar signs in the sales clerk's eyes.

I deliberately direct my attention to Grace, reminding the saleswoman that Grace is the focus here, not my mother.

Grace is studying the clothes, her expression distant. She raises a hand and runs a finger down the sleeve of the jacket, just the one finger. Like it's a piece of art she isn't certain she's allowed to touch.

We don't have time for her to admire it though. "Which one you want to try on first?" I ask. The sooner we get her into a proper suit, the sooner we can get back to all the studying she needs to do.

"Are they all my size?" Grace's hand drops, and she tries to check the tags without touching the jacket.

The sales clerk pipes up. "Mr. Tsai sent over your measurements when he asked us to bring some suits for you to look over. And of course we'll alter everything before your appointment tonight."

Grace raises an eyebrow at me. "My measurements?"

They weren't her exact measurements, just an estimate based on what I knew of her. And how much time I've spent surreptitiously studying her curves. "Just pick one," I say, "and let's get started. We still have things to do before tonight."

Alarm flashes across Grace's face and her cheeks go white. I think it's finally sinking in exactly what she's gotten into, and I almost feel bad. Just for a moment, until I ruthlessly squash it.

Grace is going to get plenty out of this. She's not a victim here, not at all.

"I guess… I guess this purple one?" Grace points to one of the suits almost randomly.

I hold in my grimace. Honestly, it's pretty hideous. The thing looks like a box made out of purple and white yarn strands—really, it's like the suits are designed to be ugly. I mean, my mother doesn't look ugly in them, but I can't imagine it suiting Grace. She's too… *light* for it.

I inwardly shake my head. That's not the point—the point is to get her through this charade.

"Ah, the lavender tweed bouclé," the saleswoman says blandly. "Good choice. It's very… timeless."

Which is a fancy way of saying old-fashioned. But maybe that's better. My mother did demand that my wife be *suitable.*

The clerk grabs the suit off the rack, takes Grace by the shoulder, and pushes her toward the bathroom in my office. Grace sends me a panicked look over her shoulder, which I meet with a stern one. She can't already be this flustered, not by a simple salesclerk. Tonight is going to be much, much worse, with my mother and sister interrogating her.

Oh shit. I haven't told my sister what's going on. Another thing to do before dinner tonight. I can't hand that call off to my assistant.

As the bathroom door slams shut behind Grace and the clerk, I grab my personal cell phone and dial Lucy. Please pick up, please pick up, I pray. If Lucy isn't in on this, she'll give it all away. She's never learned how to keep her mouth shut, and if she senses I'm up to something, she'll tattle faster than she ever did when we were kids.

Thankfully, she answers on the fourth ring.

"Brother! How are you? And congratulations on your engagement."

I'm not certain if she's referring to Amelia or Grace. I don't know what our mother's told her yet. No matter who she's referring to, she's stinking annoying. My sister was born annoying and has remained annoying. It's lucky I love her so much.

"I'm not engaged. Well, I am, kind of." I glance at the bathroom door. It seems too silent in there.

"Really? Because Mom said we were all going to meet your fiancée tonight at dinner. Which struck me as kind of odd since I've already met Amelia."

What a smart-ass. I grind my teeth. "Why didn't you stop Mother before she came all the way here with Amelia?"

That might not be fair since Lucy can't make Mother do anything, but she at least could have tried.

"Because Mom is determined to see you married," Lucy explains exasperatedly. "And when Mom is determined to do something, not even God himself can stop her. Amelia is nice. I'm sure you two will be very happy together."

"You know why I can't marry Amelia." Sometimes I think everyone in Taiwan knows about Amelia's secret affair— everyone except her parents and my mother. "I told you, I'm not proposing to her."

"Then who am I meeting tonight?"

I look again toward the bathroom door. How long does it take to put on a suit? I hope Grace doesn't want to try on multiple outfits. "Well, that kind of, sort of engagement I mentioned?" I take a deep breath although I'm not sure why. It's all fake, so there's nothing at stake in telling my sister. "It's with Grace."

I can hear my sister putting the pieces together in the pause that follows. "Grace? The one who's about to be deported? *That* Grace?"

I've mentioned Grace to Lucy before, but in passing. I didn't realize she's made that much of an impression.

"That's the one. Mother showed up and told me I had to marry Amelia—*and* announce it at the gala—and then Grace was right there, and I just…"

"You panicked?"

I scowl. "I never panic. I planned… very hastily and quickly."

"You panicked." There's a shimmer of laughter in my sister's voice. "I hope Grace told you to shove it."

I shift guiltily because Grace didn't do anything of the sort. If anything, she accepted maybe too quickly. "She said yes. It's only for a little while, until I can get Mother to drop the Amelia idea. She wants me to take over the family holdings. She says she's ready to retire."

"Yeah." My sister's voice softens. "I never thought she'd want to give all that up, but I guess it's time."

Our mother's getting older—I can feel the realization spread between us in the pause.

"She said something about the board only letting me step up if I was married," I say. "She might be stretching the truth there."

Lucy snorts. "You think? But I can see it too. The board members are kind of… older."

"Doesn't matter. They can't stop me, and there's no way I'm getting married. This engagement is just a temporary diversion."

"But you're bringing Grace to meet the family tonight." My sister pauses to let that sink in. "You're going to introduce her to everyone as if you're going to marry her. And presumably you're going to announce it at the gala. I doubt Mom gave up on that idea."

"It'll be fine. Once I'm back in Taipei, I'll say we weren't suitable or she had to stay or something." An idea begins to form in my mind. "And maybe I'll be so heartbroken over her I can't even think of marrying anyone else." I nod to myself. "That would solve a lot of problems."

Lucy sighs heavily. "It's actually insane and will never work. But if you're sure Grace is on board…"

"Grace is fine with it." And she's still not out of the bathroom. We're wasting valuable study time. "I'll make it more than worth her while financially."

"I was thinking more of the emotional fallout," my sister mutters.

I ignore that, because there won't be. We're just friends who are doing each other favors. Or maybe not even friends —we're really only connected through a friend of a friend.

The bathroom door latch snicks open, catching my attention. Grace finally comes out, wearing the purple suit. She looks…

I catch my breath because even in that fusty suit, she looks fresh and delightful. And kind of sexy to be honest. I wouldn't mind tearing the thing off her to see what racy lingerie she has on underneath.

I shake my head at myself, and Grace stumbles to a stop.

"Is it not right?" She looks so uncertain it makes my heart clench. This is going to be a lot more difficult than I thought it would be if I'm going to react to her like this.

"It's fine," I say, more bluntly than I intended. But that's okay. We both need to keep this very impersonal even if she is pretending to be the most intimate person in my life.

The phone in my hand squawks at me. Crap, I didn't hang up with my sister.

I put the phone back to my ear. "Listen, I need to finish getting her ready. I'll see you tonight at dinner."

"You're dressing her yourself?" Lucy asks. "Is that a good idea?"

I ignore that, because of course I know how to dress a woman. It's not that hard.

"It's fine," I snap. "She just has to get through dinner." I hang up then since I can't take any more crap from Lucy.

Grace is staring at me like she's never seen me before. "Is everything okay?"

I toss my phone onto my desk. "That was my sister. She knows the whole story now. How's the suit?"

Grace fingers a cuff. "It's… nice."

Great, she doesn't like it. I know what that means. "So pick another one." I force myself to smile as I wave at the rack since I'm supposed to remember my manners.

"No." She takes a step backward. "Really, it's fine. She already took the measurements to alter it."

The sales clerk appears behind Grace. "That's right. We can get started on that right away."

"I wanted to show you before I took it off," Grace says.

I let my gaze run over her, pretending to take the outfit in from all angles but really admiring the body beneath the clothes. The skirt can't hide the swells of her bottom—hell, it's hugging them.

When I look up at Grace, she's got one eyebrow raised. Like she knows exactly what I was doing.

And like maybe… she liked it.

CHAPTER SIX

It's taken us half an hour to get to the restaurant from Paul's office, and he hasn't stopped quizzing me on his many cousins the entire time.

I had no idea so many of his relatives lived here in the Bay Area. Or that they would all show up to this intimate family dinner on such short notice. Even if we are supposed to be engaged, I can't imagine his third cousin twice removed—Karen, whose parents are John and Eleanor—would ever come up between us.

But I still listen very attentively, wearing my new suit and sitting with my back straight as an arrow.

"Did you get that?" he asks irritably. "About Julian's kids? The next one is due in three months."

"I think so." He frowns at my response, so I say hastily, "Yes, I definitely did. It's just… your family is very big."

"My great-great-grandfather had three wives. It makes for a lot of cousins."

He sounds annoyed but also kind of proud. Which perhaps he should be. That all these people are willing to come together for this family occasion means something.

He also knows something about each and every one of them. How their kids are doing, what's worrying them, what to congratulate them on. His mother might be running the family enterprises, but Paul seems more than ready to lead the entire family, both in business and everywhere else.

It must also be exhausting, keeping track of all that. I'm tired and I've only spent an hour trying to get a handle on it.

"I promise I won't get it wrong," I say. "I know this is important to you."

His expression softens. "It's okay. We're kind of in the deep end here. I'm just trying to help you swim."

That's right—we're partners. Which feels strange since when he was helping me before, it wasn't a partnership. He was giving me help, and I was grateful for it. But this time if one of us fails, we both go down. The space between my heart and my stomach goes funny at that thought.

"My family isn't so big," I say. "There will be less for you to remember."

He nods. "Your father and mother are in Beijing. And no siblings. Anyone else I should know?"

I hesitate for a moment. "No, not really."

I decide not to tell him about my great-uncle. If Paul was truly my fiancé, of course I'd tell him, but… I keep thinking of my father's face when he speaks of his uncle, of exposing that pain in order to better perpetuate a lie.

I can't do it. Paul doesn't need to know that story to pretend to love me.

Paul pulls into a parking spot next to a marina. We're in East Bay now, but the most southern tip of the bay. There's a modest restaurant on the pier with windows facing the water and the boats bobbing in the slips.

The cars in the lot are anything but modest. There are Mercedes, BMWs, a Jaguar or two, and even a Rolls-Royce on one side of the lot. On the other side are Teslas, Lamborghinis, and even a Maserati. A generational divide done in automobiles, I'm guessing.

My palms start to sweat. I'm used to being around really

rich people—I've met my fair share of tech millionaires—but this is way beyond networking with Silicon Valley types. These people think I'm going to be part of their family. I have to make them *believe* I'm going to be part of their family.

Paul helps me out, his hand warm and firm as he steadies me. My heels are wobbly—the sales lady insisted I needed stilettos—so I'm grateful for his rocklike presence. I sway toward him before I can catch myself and his scent... My nerves pop and sizzle when it hits me, warm citrus and peppery undertones.

His nostrils flare as he takes a deep breath. Then another. "Your perfume," he says, all deep and low.

Oh my goodness, *we're smelling each other.* Right here in the parking lot, just breathing each other in.

His hand tightens on mine as his gaze locks on mine. My heart thumps and jumps in my chest, and I suddenly realize I'm leaning toward him. Only a few more inches and I could press my lips to his.

I snap back, locking my knees to keep from stumbling. "Sorry. Thank you," I mumble.

"It's my pleasure." His tone is back to its usual smooth politeness. But he keeps my hand in his as we walk up to the restaurant.

A note on the door announces that the restaurant is closed today for a private party. I'm a little shocked that Paul could get the entire restaurant for his family on such short notice, but I'm also not shocked. Judging by the cars in the lot, this party can afford it.

The moment we walk through the door, a young woman who looks remarkably like Paul swoops down on us. "So good to see you again!" She takes my arm as if we're old friends. "I can't wait for you to meet everyone else in the family. I keep telling Paul not to hide you away and keep you to himself. I'm glad he's finally listening to me."

"Lucy," I say, because this must Paul's sister. He told me

about her, but nothing could quite prepare me for the reality. She's dressed beautifully in a black tunic with white flowers climbing up the sleeves and sides. Her knee-high stiletto boots look brand-new without even a speck of dust.

She looks fashionable but not fussy, and pampered but not prissy. She also looks completely enthused about life.

It's kind of how I'd like to look someday, if I have the money to.

I smile at her, hoping I don't look too puzzled or like I'm trying to catch up. Which I totally am. "Well, with your mother here, Paul felt it was finally time for me to meet everyone."

"Don't worry. I won't leave you alone," Lucy says in a voice only for me. "I know it's kind of terrifying, but you've got this."

It seems Paul's not the only person in his family into rescuing people. And thank goodness for that—I'm going to need all the allies I can get.

Before we can start to make our way through the room though, everyone swarms Paul.

There's no other way to describe it; one moment Paul enters the room and the next he's surrounded by a mass of people, all of them vying for his attention. Some are telling him how good it is to see him, some are asking for his advice on investments, and others are giving him advice on investments.

He simply smiles as if this is normal, talking calmly to whoever's closest to him, working his way through the crowd.

"Wow, they really missed him," I say to Lucy.

She laughs. "No, they didn't. He saw them all two weeks ago for Jane's birthday. This is what happens every time— he's the CEO of the family, and they all want to get some face time with him."

"It looks exhausting." Not that Paul is showing even a hint of that. His smile is fixed, his expression open.

Lucy gives me a sidelong glance. "I think I'm going to like you." She takes my arm. "Come on, they won't release him for a while."

We began to make our way through the room, stopping to talk to all the cousins whose names I was supposed to have memorized. And I have—I remember enough names and details to surprise myself.

Each person we meet is friendly enough but not exactly welcoming. They keep looking past us toward Paul, as if wondering when they'll get their turn with him. He's still being swarmed, although we've already been here for twenty minutes.

Has he gotten something to eat? Or drink? Or had a chance to sit? I suppose these concerns are too wifely for me to have, but I do worry. As always, he's breathtakingly hand-some, but perhaps there's some strain there, in his forehead.

I turn away from the cousins I'm supposed to be meeting —Ruth and Ben, live in Santa Rosa, two kids, one of whom is a gifted pianist—and whisper to Lucy, "I should go check on Paul."

She looks at me like I've suggested going out to check on the car. Or maybe the clouds. "He's fine. Look"—she points to one corner of the room—"you absolutely have to meet *her*."

I know exactly who Lucy means, and my heart sinks. Still, I don't resist when she pulls me over to a young woman who's as well dressed as she is. The woman is beautiful, well groomed, sleek like a prized greyhound. And yet there's something off about her. Maybe it's the twist of her mouth and her too-tight grip on her champagne flute, but unhappi-ness seems to envelop her.

So this is the infamous Amelia. There's a tilt to her

expression that just screams nobility, at least if she ever allowed herself to do something as classless as scream.

"Amelia!" Lucy squeals. "I know you're just dying to meet Grace. Paul's fiancée."

Something flickers across Amelia's expression, something like panic and surprise mixed together. She wrestles it under control very quickly though.

I wonder if she knows she was brought here to marry Paul and if she suspects our engagement is a sham.

"I am." She holds out a slim hand for me to shake. "You're a very lucky girl. Paul's been one of Taiwan's most eligible bachelors for years now."

Then why don't you want to marry him? I don't ask it of course, but I can't imagine that whatever man she's in love with could ever compare with Paul.

"I know I am." I smile serenely, just like I imagine a princess would.

Lucy pulls us in closer together, like we're having a girls-only conversation. Her smile widens, but it's not a friendly one. "Amelia, you owe Grace a lot." Her voice drops several degrees. "I hope you don't forget it."

Suddenly I can see that Lucy isn't quite as flighty as she pretends to be. Underneath her smiling exterior lies a lioness.

Amelia's face falls. "I know that. If I could've stopped all this, I would have."

Lucy's smile never slips. "Actually, you could've if you were just honest with your parents."

Amelia looks horrified. "You know I can't do that."

"Of course not. You don't have the guts."

With that last shot, Lucy pulls me away. "Okay, now we can go rescue Paul. Not that he needs it."

I can only blink at her in shock. "I can't believe you said that."

Lucy just shrugs. "It's true. If Amelia had any kind of

backbone, this whole situation could've been avoided years ago."

"She's been in love with someone else for years?"

Lucy snags a champagne flute from a passing waiter and hands it to me. "Oh yeah. She won't give him up, and she won't tell her parents. It's a mess all around."

I couldn't imagine hiding something like that from my parents for so long. How true can their love be if their families aren't part of it?

"That's really too bad," I say as I scan the room for Paul. He's nowhere to be found though.

Instinctively my heart jumps. He wouldn't have left, not without me, but my anxiety spikes anyway. Lucy is perfectly nice and has been a great companion, but I need him.

As if he heard my thoughts, Paul appears by my side then, holding a glass of what looks like whiskey. "Sorry," he says. "I got caught up in talking to people. And then Archie wanted to chat."

Archie. That's a name I don't need to search my memory for. He's the oldest cousin and something of a thorn in Paul's side. Paul didn't give too many details, but some reading between the lines tells me that Archie wants Paul's role as head of the family.

Lucy rolls her eyes. "What's that little wannabe tyrant up to now?"

Paul sends her a scolding look. "Please don't call him that to his face. I just spent the past ten minutes convincing him I was definitely returning home to assume control. Apparently he thinks Mother is slipping."

Lucy's laugh is sharp and short. "Mom could have a lobotomy and she'd still have more business sense than Archie."

"True, but he's also close to getting a majority of the board on his side. Since I don't want to have a mutiny on my hands, I have to placate him."

Lucy makes a dismissive noise. "You're too nice to him."

Paul turns to me. "When my dad died, Archie's dad was the next oldest brother and should have taken over the company. When Mother did instead, they felt slighted. Perhaps rightfully."

"They wouldn't have done half as well as Mom did," Lucy says.

Paul takes a sip from his glass instead of answering her, his gaze running over me. I feel like I should say something —I'm guessing he'll spend all night satisfying everyone here, and I want to give him a moment of peace or laughter or something—but my voice is gone. His gaze is just that potent.

"I'll leave you two alone." Before she even finishes the sentence, Lucy turns and walks away.

I'm grateful but also nervous. If my body was just slightly less aware of his, this would be so much easier. Except my body is so, so aware of him. So alive and humming thanks to his presence that it hurts.

And he's going to be leaving soon.

"What will happen to Bastard Capital when you leave?"

He drops his gaze, his mouth pursing as he studies the floor. "Bastard Capital was for fun. Now I need to become the head of the family."

His gaze is distant and unfocused, like he's staring at a future he doesn't want. I know the exact feeling.

I take his arm because it seems like that's what I'm expected to do. I notice a few people are watching us—I'd better give them a show.

"It probably won't be so bad," I say. "You just have to keep placating wannabe tyrant Archie for the next fifty years."

He nearly chokes on his drink. "Did you really just call him that? And God forbid he lives another fifty years. He's never getting control of the company—he'd save us all a lot of trouble if he knocked it off."

He shifts, coming closer to me, our thighs brushing. A shiver runs through me.

"Speak of the devil," Paul says, looking past my shoulder, "here he comes."

I take a deep, steadying breath before I turn around, because I've still got the shivers and this will be one of the most important introductions of the night.

When I do turn, Paul immediately puts a hand to the small of my back. He's got a hint of a smile on his face, like he's looking forward to this, but the tension in the fingers pressing into my back tell the truth.

Archie looks exactly like I was expecting—plush and coddled, with a smug look that's begging for everyone to recognize how smart he is. His wife, Wendy, trails behind him. She lives in Los Angeles, and they only spend time together when Archie is here in the States. She's sleek and sharp in contrast to him, with the kind of muscles that come from long hours of careful sculpting in the gym.

His smile is wide but disingenuous; hers is small and unpleasant.

"They're clearly perfect for each other," I whisper to Paul.

He bites back a laugh as they come toward us. "Archie. Have you met Grace?"

Archie gives me a quick nod although he knows that we haven't been introduced yet. I suppose I'm not important enough for him to care about. "You left before I could finish discussing my proposal for that building in Hong Kong."

I can feel Paul internally rolling his eyes. "I'd rather not talk business tonight. We're here to meet my fiancée."

Oh crap. Their attention focuses fully on me. I keep my polite princess expression on even as I lean into Paul's hand.

Archie's wife swivels her head toward me. The gesture makes chills run over my skin. "How did you two meet? No one in the family's mentioned you before." Her head tilts. "Not even Paul."

I freeze even though that's the worst possible reaction. I know we came up with a backstory, somewhere between all the quizzes about his family, but it's not coming to me.

"I'm involved with a start-up he invested in," I say. I think that's what we decided on, and it's not exactly a lie. It's also not very convincing.

Paul slides his hand around my back to my waist, pulling me into the curve of his body. Again his scent makes my brain scramble. "It's not a very exciting story, I'm afraid. We spent some time together, and I simply realized…" He looks deep into my eyes, his lips parting slightly. He looks… enchanted. A prince coming under a spell. "I realized she was the one. That I couldn't spend my life without her."

He's an excellent liar, and I almost believe him myself. He's looking at me like he can't wait to get me alone. I can feel my cheeks heating. Thankfully his family won't expect us to be too physically affectionate since it's bad manners, but in that moment, I can almost imagine him kissing me senseless. A kiss to put a seal on our hearts.

And after that kiss, he'd kiss me to open my body entirely to him—

I clear my throat, hard. "I think our story is romantic. Paul's a very charming man. He can make any situation feel special."

Like he's doing right now.

"Hmm" is all Wendy says, and I can already see what she's thinking—*gold digger*.

Well, considering what Paul's going to pay me for my time, I guess she's not wrong.

"Your mother says you're going to announce your engagement at the gala." Archie nods approvingly. "That's good PR. Smart of you to think of it."

Paul smiles indulgently. "It was actually Mother's idea. I wanted a simple announcement for just the family, but she's always thinking about what's best for the company."

Archie goes a rather angry shade of red. Probably because Paul's just called him out for his rude words about Paul's mother, albeit in a very subtle way.

There are some sputtering noises from Archie, which Paul ignores. Instead, he points to the head table. "Speaking of Mother, we really should chat with her," he says.

His hand around my waist squeezes, as if I'm in for the best gift ever when we talk to her.

Archie's wife assumes an exaggerated expression of surprise. "When did your mother meet her? I thought she just flew in."

"Only briefly at the office earlier." Paul isn't a bit fazed. "Mother came straight from the airport."

Archie looks way too pleased with himself for my taste. "Too bad you'll have to leave all this kid stuff behind when you go home for good. But we all have to grow up sometime."

As if what Paul does here is playing around. I can feel my chest puffing up with indignation on Paul's behalf.

I'm half tempted to snap at Archie, but instead I put on that serene smile that I've been practicing. "Paul's very good at managing his time," I say. "I'm sure he'll be able to handle running the family holdings and doing whatever else he wants on the side. Most people can't manage that, or much of anything"—I give Archie a cold look—"but he can."

Before Archie can react, Paul leads me away. Oh crap, I think I might have gone a bit too far. I'm supposed to be ingratiating myself with the family, not antagonizing them.

But Paul's expression is admiring and a little surprised. My heart lifts when I see it. "Maybe you know how to deal with Archie even better than I do."

"I doubt that."

Paul takes me slowly, steadily toward his mother. Other family members try to catch his eye, but he ignores them.

I wish I had his poise. I'm about to meet his mother again.

Freaking out doesn't even begin to describe what my insides are doing.

But I keep my smile on my face because Paul is counting on me. I've come this far; I can do this.

She's sitting at the head of the table, watching over the family as they eat. Whereas everyone was swarming Paul and demanding his attention, the family keeps a respectful distance around her. No one is going to demand anything from this woman. She's beyond that.

Even though all this is fake, I still desperately want to pass her inspection. What woman wouldn't want to be deemed worthy of marrying Paul?

Paul approaches her respectfully but not deferentially. Based on the light in his eyes, he really does love his mom. She's not exactly warm and fuzzy, but there's definitely affection between them.

She turns her sharp gaze on me, waiting.

"Mother, I wanted you and Grace to have a chance to get to know each other." Paul brings me one step closer to her.

I bow, trying to make it as elegant and respectful as possible.

His mother says nothing, continuing to inspect me very, very carefully.

I can't blame her, to be honest. I think she might actually be right about Paul needing a wife as he assumes control of the family holdings. If Cousin Archie is any indication, there are some people who are going to have it in for Paul. He's going to need someone trustworthy at his back.

It won't be me of course, but he still deserves that person.

"So you're the woman my son's going to marry." It's not a question, and it's not welcoming. Already I can see she has her doubts about all this.

"Yes," I say quietly, my eyes downcast. "I hope to make him a good wife."

A small smile toys at the edges of her mouth. I suspect

she's guessed what I'm doing, that my answer is as practiced as her expression.

"Have you met everyone yet?"

"Oh yes. Everyone's been so kind."

His mother makes a noise that sounds suspiciously like a snort, only way more ladylike. "I'm certain they were. You understand that Paul is going to be returning home soon? That he'll be taking over a very great responsibility?"

She's not wasting time with subtlety, which I actually appreciate. Paul has important duties, and she wants to make sure I understand those duties.

"Yes, we've discussed it. Paul's very eager to take his place as head of the family, and I want to help him any way I can."

That's not entirely a lie: I'm here, lying to this woman, in order to help Paul. I find myself wishing I could get the chance to explain that to her once our charade is done.

But I won't. She'll likely despise me if she ever discovers the truth. She definitely won't be happy when I "leave" her son in a few weeks.

"And your job here?" she asks. "Won't you be upset to leave it?"

This is not the time and place to mention that I'm unemployed and about to lose my visa. "If—when—I marry Paul, that will be my job. Being his wife."

Her expression flickers like she's displeased. But I thought the whole point of Paul having to marry was to have a wife entirely focused on him.

"When is the wedding?" she asks.

"We haven't set a date yet," Paul says. "I have to plan the move back to Taipei first."

"And when is that happening?" his mother asks sharply.

"Soon." Paul's tone gets a little cold, a little hard. "I can't just up and leave at a moment's notice."

His mother closes her eyes very briefly. It might have been a simple blink, but she held it just a bit too long. She looks almost tired. Or at least as tired as she'll allow herself to be.

"Paul understands that he needs to return home soon," I say quickly.

Paul gives me a surprised look, as if he wasn't expecting me to jump in. But he doesn't seem to be taking his mother's request that seriously.

"That's right," he says. "You'll be able to retire very soon, I promise. And I'll do an excellent job running the company. I won't let it fail. I won't let this family fail."

When he says that, the assembled people seem to take on a weight, one that settles right on Paul's shoulders. *This family* refers to everyone in this room. And everyone I haven't met back in Taiwan. All those people are Paul's personal responsibility.

His mother's expression eases, then shifts into something resolute. "No, you won't."

It's not comforting, it's not reassuring—and I'm not sure it's what Paul needs to hear.

CHAPTER SEVEN

For the first time in two hours, I don't have someone clamoring for my attention. I'm taking advantage by sitting in a corner and watching Grace as she charms my oldest aunt.

She's been amazing tonight. And she looks amazing. She did something with her hair, twisting it up and putting orchids in it, that makes me want to undo it, flowers falling to the floor as her hair spreads over her bare shoulders—

"Chanel?" Lucy says, scaring the shit out of me as she takes the chair next to me. "How terribly predictable. It doesn't suit her at all."

"Did you see me enjoying myself and decide to ruin it?"

Lucy turns a serious expression on me. "I really like her. And you need to let her dress herself."

"Grace looks fine." We both watch her as she chats with Auntie May. "She looks…"

The words that come to me aren't really words—more like sensations. A strand of hair has slipped free of her updo and is caressing her neck, her cheeks are flushed, and she's laughing at something May has said, which all comes together to make her sparkle. How am I supposed to notice what she's wearing when the rest of her is so beautiful?

Lucy clicks her tongue. "Chanel is for old ladies and

young women edgy enough to pull off that stodgy look. Grace needs to be in something… very different. Something sweeter."

"High fashion that's sweet?" I check out Lucy's dress, which is in stark shades of white and black, and boots with heels that could kill a man. "You're out of your mind."

My sister sighs heavily. "It's really sad how little you know about women." She ignores my spluttering protest. "I'll take her shopping. I'll fix all this."

I've been busting my ass all night convincing my family that Grace and I are madly in love, but my sister's going to "fix all this." Right.

"Be my guest. I didn't have much time today, what with Mother showing up unannounced." And finding a fake fiancée and tutoring her in our long family history and getting this entire dinner together. But of course my annoying sister zeros in on the most unimportant aspect of the whole thing.

Lucy taps her nails against the table. They're long, dark red, and fake—and something our mother would hate.

"Don't get Grace that kind of manicure though," I say, pointing to her nails.

Lucy examines them, smiling as she does. "They really did come out gorgeous. But no, Grace needs something shorter, maybe in a dark berry." Lucy's head swings up, her gaze catching on Amelia. Her eyes narrow in a way I can only call mean.

Which is confusing, because Amelia and Lucy have always been friendly, if not friends.

"What?" I ask.

"Amelia's not too happy about this whole thing." Lucy doesn't look away from her.

I study Amelia myself. She looks like she always does. "I don't know what you mean. She's been fine as far as I can tell."

My sister shakes her head. "No, Amelia is about to crack. This secret affair's been going on too long. She needs to tell her family the truth or end it, but she's too much of a coward to do either."

"Amelia's not a coward," I instinctively say. She's always been fragile though. Which suddenly strikes me as completely ridiculous considering all the advantages she's had in life. What the hell does Amelia have to be fragile about?

My sister rolls her eyes. "Of course she is. And because she *is* a coward, she'd make a terrible wife for you."

"That's not what you said—"

Lucy ignores me, her attention focusing on Grace. "Now Grace—"

"I'm not marrying her." It's out of the question, and if my sister's got matchmaking designs, she can quit it right now. "It's ending when I leave or she does—that's the whole point of the scheme. It's not to get married."

"It could become real though."

"You need to stop watching so many K-dramas. They're pickling your brain."

She reaches out and swats me. "My brain is just fine. I'll have you know that I recently got a massive grant renewal, all thanks to my brain."

My sister, in addition to be annoying and vivacious and flighty, is also a world-famous scientist. She has a lab of her own at UCSF and everything. I'm not entirely sure what she studies—when she starts talking, it sounds like Mongolian to me—but everyone is always exclaiming over what a genius she is.

I have to admit I'm pretty proud of her and what she's achieved, not that I'd ever tell her that. At least not unless I was on my deathbed.

"Grace just has this... poise," my sister goes on. "And you... you *like* her."

I suck in a breath. Of course I like Grace—but Lucy means something different. Deeper.

I'm attracted to Grace. And I fall deeper and deeper into it every time I see her. Which means I'm going to be out of mind with lust by the time this ends.

I close my eyes and sigh. The trouble isn't going to be pretending to be crazy about Grace—the trouble will come when I try to get her out of my system once this is over.

Answering Lucy would be useless. Because I do like Grace and I can't.

Lucy keeps on going though. "I think Mom suspects something's up."

"Yeah, I noticed that," I say dryly. "But at least she's not talking about my marrying Amelia anymore."

Lucy pulls the exact same face she did when we were kids and she couldn't get a second dessert. She'd ask for a second dessert, get told no, then keep on asking. See what I mean about being annoying?

"Is Grace really going to be deported?"

Yeah, she is. And I don't think there's a damn thing I can do about it. "Immigration is insisting on it, so yes."

"I thought those H-1B visas were easy to transfer. Whenever we do it, it's not so bad."

Sweet, innocent Lucy. No one in academic science ever wants to punish their ex-employees through the immigration system. "They're actually not that easy to transfer. But when your former employer is a complete asshole with the ears of the highest levels of government, it gets much, much tougher."

Grace is rising, offering Auntie May her arm. Auntie May's probably ready to go home. Before I can step in and summon her driver, Grace is gesturing to him with her free hand. With a smile and a final bow, Grace hands Auntie May over to the man. I can't remember when I last saw Auntie May smile like that.

It's a simple thing, making sure my Auntie May leaves safely, but those little things matter. The family needs someone looking after those little things as much as the big ones.

Lucy raises an eyebrow when she catches me staring after Grace. "See? You've got that look again."

"We're pretending to be engaged." But I force myself to look away. Grace said goodbye to my aunt, that's all. She's pretending here too.

"You've never been that good of a liar," Lucy says.

"Watch me." I catch Grace's eye and crook a finger at her. We've done enough faking tonight—it's high time we went home. "I've already got you believing, don't I?"

With that, I leave my annoying sister behind and go to rejoin my temporary fiancée.

CHAPTER EIGHT

By the time we say our goodbyes to the last family member and make our way to the parking lot, I'm barely holding in my yawns. I had no idea pretending was going to be such tiring work. I guess actors really do earn those paychecks.

Paul, in contrast, looks as crisp as ever. He ushers me into the car with perfect grace and charm, smiling as if he's secretly looking forward to the rest of our evening, although no one's out here to see. I suppose it doesn't hurt to be too careful though.

I let my head fall against the soft leather headrest, eager for my bed. Was it really just this morning that I had the interview at Pixio? It's like I've lived several lifetimes since then. At least I can sleep in tomorrow. In fact, if Paul hadn't given me the job of pretending to adore him, I wouldn't have much of anything to do for the next few weeks besides pack up my things.

"You all right?" he asks as he swings the car out into traffic.

I sit up straight. "I'm fine."

"You did this… sigh." A note vibrates low and deep in his voice.

"I'm just tired. It's been a long day." I'm tempted to ask

him if I did okay, but that would feel too much like begging for his approval. I'd like to hear that I did well, of course, but I want him to freely offer that praise.

And I want to know that his family was convinced that I was good enough for him. Being confronted with his mother's choice of a bride rattled me a bit. Amelia didn't impress me exactly, but there's no denying she's more beautiful, more elegant, than I could ever be.

I don't know what to make of Amelia. I suspect Lucy's right about her, that she's weak. I suppose I should feel sorry for her, but I can't be *that* sorry. Amelia has all the money in the world, and maybe if she actually tried speaking with her parents instead of hiding her true feelings, she might be a happier person.

Of course, I also understand the importance of family. If I were in love with someone my father wouldn't approve of, I'm not sure if I would tell him either. Actually, I don't think I'd ever date someone my family didn't approve of. I certainly haven't until now.

Now I'm lying to one of the richest, most powerful families in the world. And unless I tell my parents the truth, I'll be lying to them too.

I let my gaze run over Paul, who's concentrating on the road. His forehead is stern—traffic is heavy—but his lips remain soft. It would take a great deal of anger to make his lips hard, I think.

Would my father approve of Paul? It doesn't matter since our engagement is fake anyway, but now that I've asked the question, I want an answer.

Paul has excellent manners, comes from a very respectable family, and perhaps that would be enough for my father. But Paul is also lying to his mother without much guilt. That's a definite strike against him.

"Thank you for taking care of Auntie May," Paul says without looking at me.

"I didn't do anything, simply called her driver and then helped her to him. Anyone could have done it." I had noticed him in the corner, taking a break from the incessant demands of his family. May had wanted to go interrogate him on some detail of her personal investments, but I distracted her with small talk until she was ready to go home. Paul deserved to keep that moment of peace without any interruptions.

"Hmm." He sounds as if he doesn't quite believe that, but I don't see why. "How was meeting the infamous Lillian Tsai?"

He's mocking me, but it's gentle. "Your mom scares me. In a good way." I look out the window at the scenery blurring by. "I don't think I fooled her."

Paul laughs humorlessly. "No, she's not going to be easily convinced. But I haven't had to propose to Amelia yet, so our plan is working so far."

I keep my head turned away as my chest pinches. My feelings shouldn't be involved, but it still hurts that he isn't more… effusive about my efforts tonight. I'm doing this as a favor to him—I thought I did fairly well with limited resources and on such short notice. I'm not going to win any acting awards, but he could be a little bit more appreciative.

The silence between us spreads, adjusting itself until it fills the entirety of the car. I guess we don't have much to talk about since we're not talking about my immigration situation, but the silence still feels awkward and wrong.

We're supposed to be engaged. We don't have to pretend to love each other right now, but shouldn't we at least be practicing for the real thing?

"What pets did you have as a kid? And which did you love best?" I ask out of the blue.

Paul's head snaps over in surprise. "Pets?"

"Yes. I know the name of your fifth cousin twice removed, but I don't know anything about *you*. We didn't talk about your cousins on our fake dates."

He drums his fingers against the steering wheel, then stills them. "I didn't have any pets. My mother thought it unfair to add to the servants' duties."

Oh. That's horrible. I swallow, trying to think of something to say beyond *How sad*. And it's so uniquely horrible, so very poor little rich boy.

"We had a cat," I say instead, brightly. "She was a calico with patches of white and orange and black. She always seemed very proud of her looks, but I suppose she had the right. She was very pretty."

His expression is reluctantly curious, like he wants to ask more but doesn't want to seem too interested in a cat. "Is she still alive?"

"No, she passed away right before I left for university. My parents were so heartbroken they couldn't bear to replace her. Her favorite cushion still sits on the window ledge." A notebook of my great-uncle's poems sits on the table next to the window, both reminders of beloved things my family lost and continues to mourn.

"I'm sorry," he says with deep sincerity.

"Thank you," I reply, just as sincere. There's a beat of silence, but this time it's more comfortable. Lived in. "I should probably also know your favorite color. Your aunt May wanted to buy some shirts for you, and she was asking which color would be best." I nibble on my lower lip. "I didn't know your birthday was coming up."

He closes his eyes for a moment. "Shit. I forgot to tell you about that."

"It's okay. I was able to fake that I knew it."

"Wait… what color did you tell her?"

"Oh, I said that safety orange would be best. That I was inspiring you to be more daring with your fashion choices."

There's a moment of shocked quiet. "You… you're joking?"

I snort. "Of course. As if your aunt would ever believe I could inspire you to something like that."

The look he sends me is intense, burning. But only for an instant, and then he's back to unflappable Paul. "Maybe you should come stay at my place. Then we'll have more time to go over details like this before the gala."

My cheeks go red hot. I'm not prudish, but the thought of sharing a space, even platonically, makes my skin ignite. And not just with embarrassment.

"That's not really necessary," I stammer. "What would your mother think?"

"Do you really care what my mother thinks? Besides, she'll never find out. You can't really be scared of her."

"Not scared exactly. But your mom is pretty freaking amazing. You know that, don't you?"

"Of course I do." His tone is grim. "Which is why I'm going through all this, so I can take over the company but not have to marry Amelia."

I wonder who he'll end up marrying. Probably someone like Amelia, only without the secret long-term love affair. Born to his exclusive world of privilege and wealth, who won't have to memorize his fifth cousin twice removed because she'll have already known them her entire life.

He won't have to pretend with her.

"I'm not comfortable lying to your mother any more than necessary," I say stiffly.

He catches my implied criticism—he's clearly fine with lying to his mother all over the place—and his expression shutters. "You have to decide soon if you're coming home with me. The turnoff is coming up."

I have no idea where he lives. I suppose I could've found out in one of the many fawning profiles of him in the Asian papers, but I never read them. I was trying to not feed my obsession.

Considering how frosty the atmosphere is between us, I won't have to worry about that.

"If you think it best…"

"I do," he says shortly. "Otherwise I wouldn't have suggested it. Don't worry, I'm not going to tell anyone. Your reputation is safe."

My mouth purses. He makes me sound like some kind of shrinking virgin. I was only thinking about his mother and how she would take it.

And maybe a little bit about my own weakness when it comes to him and how I'm going to survive that much closeness. But we're faking being engaged—you can't get much closer than that. I can handle sleeping under the same roof. And I'm guessing his roof is pretty big.

I also want to prove to him that I don't care, that staying at his place is no big deal.

"Okay," I say offhandedly. "But I'll need to get my things."

"Don't worry about it. Lucy is going to take you shopping tomorrow. Apparently I picked out all the wrong things."

So that's the real reason he's irritated—his little sister insulted him. I suppose Paul can't wear his polite mask all the time, but I never imagined it could be like this. It's not off-putting—more like a juicy secret only I'm allowed to know. Paul Tsai, superbillionaire and heir to one of the finest families in Asia, can also be persnickety. It's cute.

No, I'm not using *that* word. Cute is dangerous. Cute is intimate, the word a woman uses when she knows a man way too well. Cute is not what I get to call Paul.

I clear my throat, getting any lingering bit of *cute* out. "I like Lucy."

Paul smiles, his expression filled with affection and exasperation. "God, she's so annoying. But she seems to like you too."

I don't have a sister, and Paul's obvious love for his makes my chest ache. Lucy would be a great sister to have, and I kind of wish she could be mine. Only that will never happen.

"She doesn't seem to like Amelia," I say carefully. I'm watching his reaction much too closely.

He blinks, but that's all. "Hmm." It's not a warning, exactly, but it lets me know I'm treading too close to an area I shouldn't.

Fine. We don't have to discuss the woman his mother really wants him to marry. None of my business.

Except maybe it kind of is since he pulled me into all this. But I let it drop.

"Where am I supposed to appear next?" I can't keep the trepidation out of my voice. Tonight was survivable but not exactly fun.

He sighs. With class, but it's still a sigh. "I'm hoping everyone will be too busy getting ready for the gala to do another family dinner."

I frown. "But the gala is three weeks away. They're going to take that long to get ready for a party?"

He sends me a sardonic look. "They've spent all year getting ready for this party. The second they leave the opera house, they're already planning their dresses for next year. And how to outdo whichever rival pissed them off that year."

I'd say that it sounds like a K-drama, except I have to live through it somehow. "Sounds fun."

"It's not that bad. We raise a lot of money, and the food is always… decent."

"Don't oversell it," I say dryly. "Backstabbing with a side of mediocre food. What's not to love?"

He starts laughing again, almost against his will. "When did you get such a smart mouth?"

I've always had it, but it's not something I bring out for just anyone. I guess I feel comfortable enough with him to be sarcastic. Or maybe I need to release the pressure of this charade though snarky remarks. "Don't worry. I won't be smart with your mother. Or any of your other relatives."

The grin he sends warms me from the inside out. Overheats me, really. "Oh no, you have to do this for Lucy. She'll be so disappointed if she doesn't get to see this side of you."

He gets off the freeway at the 84, going west instead of east, taking us up and up into the forested hills of Woodside.

"You live up here?" I ask. Woodside is mostly rural, at least rural as far as billionaires define it. It's mostly twenty-acre lots with stables and swing sets and private hiking trails. It's for families, not dashing bachelors like Paul. Superrich families, but still families.

"It's more private out here." He shrugs. "I like having a space that's all my own, that no one else can get close to."

"Kind of like a castle with a moat."

He looks puzzled at the reference. "I suppose so. But no dragons."

We drive for some time, going higher and higher into the hills until there are very few signs of civilization. Finally we turn in to an unmarked driveway protected by massive wrought iron gates. Paul doesn't have to punch in a code; the gates just open automatically for us.

Although it's dark, I get the impression of massive trees lining the drive, blocking out anything that might be beyond them. I guess Paul wasn't joking when he said he valued his privacy. There's literally nothing else around us, but he still feels the need to screen his driveway from view.

The drive up to the house feels endless, and not just because I'm nervous. This really is a long driveway.

When the lights of the house come into view, I'm almost disappointed. From what I can see, it looks like a smallish, single-story house. Not at all what I imagined him living in. Which is a silly thought because I really don't care what his house looks like.

I'm just about to compliment him on how nice his house

is when there's a blaze of light. Someone's flicked on all the switches inside the house, lighting up each and every window. I can suddenly see the place for what it really is—massive and luxurious. There are three stories, at least two wings and multiple balconies.

I'm trying not to stare, but it's hard. Paul drives us around the back, pulling into an immaculate garage with a parquet floor. There's a Rolls-Royce and an antique Jaguar already sitting in the garage.

He helps me out and leads me through a door. I have to gasp when I see what's on the other side. "Do you really have *two* pools?"

Paul grimaces. "The previous owner did it. I guess his wife liked to swim in water that was cooler and he liked it warmer. So two pools. The cold one makes for a nice plunge after the sauna, you know."

I nod like I do, even though having my own private cold-water bath for after my own private sauna session is something I've never, ever imagined. I mean, I've certainly gone to the common baths and even the hot springs in Longxi, which are supposed to be therapeutic, but it was always a communal experience. Communal isn't bad, but private sounds much better.

"How nice," I say. "That *is* convenient."

I'm not trying to be snarky, not really, but Paul makes a wry gesture with his hand. "Sorry, I know it's ridiculous, but I guess I've kind of gotten used to it. Even I think two pools is too much, but I didn't see the sense in tearing one out."

"But what if you need another tennis court?"

"Well—" He blinks at me. His refined confusion is adorable. "You're making a joke."

"No, I'm serious. What if you like to play tennis on a hard court and your wife wants to play on clay? It's a dilemma for the ages."

"I do have a tennis court, but just the one. You know, like a peasant."

I have to laugh at that because in no way is Paul a peasant. I don't think he's ever even met a peasant, except for me. "What about stables? Do you have two stables?"

His expression turns sheepish. "There are two barns, yes. My sister keeps her horses here too. So we needed the space."

I stop before the door he's holding open for me. "*Her* horses too? There are his and hers horses here?"

He gestures me forward, the sweep of his hand curt. "Yes. I've always enjoyed riding, so I made sure the house had stables."

One set of stables is an extravagance, but two? There weren't many horses where I grew up, and I've always been a bit afraid of them. So big, with so many teeth. And their feet perfect for crushing toes with.

He's leading us through the back way. I'm not sure if this is a compliment or an insult. I'm not grand enough to enter through the front door, but maybe it's because I'm trusted enough to go through the back. I get the impression that this is Paul's usual route into the house.

But even for the back way it's very impressive. We pass a kitchen that could serve an army, a home theater with rows of plush velvet seats, and a room that's just filled with flower arrangements. Some chairs and tables, yes, but mostly flower arrangements.

I have never before heard of a house with a flower arrangement appreciation room. I didn't even think such a thing could exist.

We emerge into the front hallway. No, the entrance hallway. No…

My brow furrows as I try to put a name on what this is. It takes up all three stories, ending in a rotunda that's painted with a sunset sky, pinks and golds and deep blue, with clouds streaking through it. This is… beyond impressive. I

know my mouth is hanging open, but I can't help it. It's…
palatial.

"That came with the house too," Paul says as an aside.

Several uniformed maids come scurrying to meet us, mild panic in their eyes.

"What the hell is going on?" Paul asks. "Why are you wearing your uniforms?"

One of the maids comes forward. "Your mother called to say she'll be arriving in an hour and to prepare her usual room. We thought it best…"

Paul rolls his eyes toward the ceiling. "Son of a bitch. No, you were right to put them on." He turns to me. "We'll have to hide you."

Hide me? From what? "I don't understand…"

"My mother's decided to stay here instead of at the hotel. Which means the maids have to be in their proper uniform and you have to be nowhere to be found. She won't like us living together before we're married."

This is so surreal it's head-spinning. We're lying to his mother about all this, and now we have to lie about my staying here? "I guess I'm going to the pool house then."

This place probably has two pool houses. I'll have my choice of them.

Paul shakes his head. "She'll notice if someone's living in the pool house. But there's…" His gaze runs over me, and suddenly my skin feels too tight for my body. When his eyes meet mine again, there's a strange, savage spark, like his skin also feels too tight.

I swallow hard and try to think of cold, hard objects, like stones or glass or similarly unfeeling things.

"You're not going to like this," he says. "You're really not going to like this."

"Is it the servants' quarters?" They're probably nicer than my own apartment.

A smile dances at the edge of Paul's mouth, which he

ruthlessly tries to suppress. "No, you're not sleeping in the attic. But there are some guest quarters in my wing of the house. My mother would have to go through my rooms to access it, and even as nosy as she is, I can't imagine her invading my space."

Okay, now my skin is *really* too tight. "I'm going to be… I'm going to stay in your rooms? Like, rooms plural?" I asked hopefully.

We're not staying in the same bed. We're not staying in the same room. I keep chanting that in my head to calm myself.

"There are multiple beds, don't worry. But it will be tight quarters." His expression is quite serious.

I imagine my definition of tight quarters is very different from his. There's probably a whole suite of rooms back there, attached to his even bigger suite of rooms. Entire villages could probably live in what he calls tight quarters.

"Okay," I said quickly. "It's fine, really."

"Should I take your bags?" a maid asks me. I've almost forgotten they were there, they were so quiet.

"She doesn't have any bags," Paul says. "Could you show her upstairs?"

He leaves before the maid can respond, already expecting her to say yes.

When we arrive, I see that I was right—tight quarters means something very different to Paul. There's a sitting room, a bedroom, a walk-in closet, and a bathroom that's covered in marble.

I flop down on the bed, letting my purse fall to the floor. I'm exhausted, but my brain is going too fast to allow me to sleep. And I've got nothing else to do but to wait for Paul to come back. I can't go exploring, and TV doesn't appeal.

But I can call January and tell her everything. I pull out my phone, automatically checking my email before I do anything else. Without a job, there's really no point—no one's trying to contact me after hours for anything important—but the habit is too hard to break.

When I see the email waiting for me, my skin goes as cold as if I've jumped into one of Paul's pools.

From: Arne Fuchs

Subject: Immigration Issues

Tell me who the leak is at Corvus and I'll make all your visa problems go away.

I should have known Mother would be too classy to go looking under the bed for Grace.

She arrived, looking tired, just after I sent Grace upstairs. It made me frown because she used to handle jet leg as if it didn't exist. My mother never slows down for anything, not even time zone changes.

After wishing me a good night, she immediately went to bed. No interrogating me about Grace, badgering me about taking over the company, or asking what Archie was up to at dinner, which was what I'd braced myself for.

Nope, she just took off, and I weirdly feel guilty. Like she's tired, worn out, and here I am lying to her.

I manage to get over it though as I go upstairs to find Grace. The servants know better than to say anything, so our secret is safe for now. Just another few weeks to get through, then Grace will be home and so will I.

My foot falters on the step. Thinking of Taipei as home is… not wrong, but this place is home too. I'm going to miss the Bay Area and especially the Bastards. And the man I could be with them—a little freer, looser, happier.

Of course I'm happy to return home and do my duty. I shake my head. I can't go down this path. My life was decided the second I was born. This was only an interlude, and I've always known that. An interlude that's left its mark on me but has to end.

I find Grace in her room, looking out at the pool. The colder one.

The light from the water ripples over her features, high-lighting her eyes, then her cheeks, then the lush curves of her mouth. Something about her stillness makes me slow, then stop, the better to appreciate the sight. Gorgeous is too weak a word for her.

I've noticed how beautiful she was before, but I wouldn't let myself admit it. But now, watching her like this, I can't do anything *but* notice.

She catches me watching and the moment dissolves. Her smile is apologetic, like I've caught her doing something she shouldn't.

"Which pool is that?" she asks.

"The cold one. You'll want to swim in the other pool."

"I don't have a suit."

"Lucy already called Saks and asked for some clothes to be sent over. They should arrive first thing tomorrow morning."

"That was really nice of her." She twists her hands together, like she's trying to rub away a stain.

"Is everything okay?" I come to her side, stopping myself before I put a hand on her shoulder. She might be upset because of me, actually. That dinner wasn't exactly relaxing, and now she's hiding out from my mother.

"Um." Her mouth twists like she's struggling with what to say.

Great. My family ruined her evening, but she's afraid to tell me that. "You don't have to say anything," I say. "I can just go."

"No." She takes my forearm to stop me. I can't help but

stare at her hand, pale against the pearl gray of my shirt. "It's something else. Fuchs emailed me."

That asshole. The tension builds in my head as my blood pressure spikes. "What did he say? If he threatened you, we're going straight to the police. I don't care if he's bought them too. And we'll get you a security detail, twenty-four seven. I should have already thought of that."

Her tongue darts out to wet her lips. "That's very… thorough of you, but he wants to make a deal. I expose his leak and he fixes my visa issues."

I blink at her for a long moment, processing that. We discovered the mole within Corvus about two weeks ago, when they sent some explosive information to Finn and Doc. Grace then helped the two of them plant a virus in Corvus's servers that killed a police surveillance program, one that was being used to lock up innocent people.

"Son of a bitch," I mutter. "I told Finn to keep you out of it, and now Fuchs is coming after you. Again."

Although, since he's done his best to get her deported, there's not much else Fuchs can do to her. The strange thing is, once she's out of the country, she'll probably be pretty safe from him. I mean, China has its own intense, invasive surveillance programs, but they're not run by Corvus.

Fuchs can still use her though, which is what he's trying to do.

She shrugs. "I don't know if he suspects I helped with the virus. I think if he did, he wouldn't have made the offer. He's not the forgiving type."

"No, I didn't get that impression. So, do you even know who the leak is? And how would he know to contact you about it?"

Maybe Fuchs is just fishing, seeing if Grace knows anything. He must suspect how desperate she is at this point to stop her deportation.

"You guys are helping me, January rescued me, and she's

already trying to shut down his spyware program." She raises her eyebrow. "If there is a leak in the company, you guys are in the best position to use that info to hurt him."

"If? We know for certain there is one."

She nods. "And he must too. So he figures I'll weasel the identity of the mole out of you guys. Or just give it up if I already know it." She takes a deep breath. "He's put me in this awful position, and now he's using it for leverage."

I take her hand, squeeze hard. "If you can figure out who it is, just give it to him. You don't owe that person anything." My heart is beating hard, harder than it should be.

Because I'm too invested in this? In keeping her here?

I drop her hand. It doesn't matter because I'm leaving myself. Grace's future and mine are not intertwined.

"Denounce them?" She looks like I just asked her to execute them publicly.

"When did I say denounce?" Jesus, that wasn't what I meant at all. "You give Fuchs the name and all your problems are gone."

"And the leaker's problems?" She's working herself up, which I can't understand. "What happens to them?"

"They're probably a citizen and they'll be fine."

"Would you hire them?"

I hesitate for a moment, because of course I wouldn't. Yes, they might have made it possible for us to screw Fuchs, but they're still disloyal. I'm not Fuchs—for one thing, I have a soul—but I wouldn't knowingly hire a leaker even if they'd helped me before.

Grace pounces on my hesitation. "See? They'd be fired, disgraced, and even you wouldn't help them."

I pinch the bridge of my nose. "You're about to be deported. And you're throwing away the best chance you have to stop this?"

She purses her lips, pain bracketing her mouth. She sits heavily in a chair, like she can't stand a moment longer. "I… I just don't know if I can betray someone like that." Tears shine in her eyes. "I probably should have told you before, but my great-uncle was a dissident."

I close my eyes. Shit. I should have guessed at something like that. Of course she would hate surveillance, would be horrified at being involved in it, would fight to stay here. "What happened?"

"Nothing that dramatic. He was a poet. He wrote about…" Her mouth twists wryly. "About everything he saw. But some things weren't supposed to be mentioned, although he did anyway. He was warned, he kept writing his poetry, and he was arrested and sentenced. He died in prison."

I take a knee next to her, wrapping my hands around hers. They're small and cold, and I try to rub some warmth, some comfort into them. "You didn't have to tell me. But I understand now."

"That's not all. My father… he loved his uncle very much. And when he had to denounce this man he respected and honored so deeply—something broke in my father, I think. From then on, he urged me to leave." She sniffles, a small, slight sound that still tears at my heart. "So I tried my hardest to come here."

Christ, this is one tangled situation. Of course she can't let her parents down—or herself—by blowing this opportunity to remain… but she can't betray them either by exposing someone else.

"We'll… we'll tell Fuchs you have no idea who the leak is." It's a weak response, but I can't come up with anything better. "And maybe he'll be inclined to drop it."

She smiles like she doesn't believe me, but my effort touched her anyway. "He won't. And I could look through what the leaker sent to Finn and Doc. I might be able to figure out who it is."

I hold my breath because I can't quite believe it. "You're going to give him the name?"

She shakes her head. "No. I don't know. But at least I can go through the files, see what's there. I can meet with him, see what he's willing to offer."

It's all very logical and exactly what she ought to do, but the thought of her dealing with Fuchs is making my blood burn. But hell, she doesn't have a choice anymore. I and all my fancy lawyers have failed her. Fuchs is the only chance she has left.

I swallow. "I'll arrange a meeting with Finn and Doc tomorrow morning. From there, we'll go see Fuchs. Together."

"Right." She nods like she's trying to convince herself. "It's silly to think this is anything like what happened to my great-uncle. I need to just deal with it. I *will* just deal with it."

Her bravery... I can't quite describe what it does to me since I've never experienced a sensation like this before. Life keeps throwing shit at her—clods of it—and she keeps dodging it with a grace I've never imagined.

"What's your name?" I ask. "Your real name."

I don't mean Grace, the name she probably picked in some English class. I mean the one her parents gave her.

She looks confused at the change of subject but answers anyway. "Zhenzhen."

Precious. It suits her. Grace suits her too.

"You don't have to deal with it alone." I suddenly realize I'm still holding her hands.

"I know." Her eyes are like the clearest pools, and I want to drown in them. "You've been so kind—"

I don't want to hear that shit. I haven't been kind at all, or noble, or any of the other things I was raised to be. So I kiss her.

She makes a noise, more like a breath, a sigh against my mouth. Something in my midsection unknots at the touch of her lips to mine. A little piece of resistance I didn't even know was there.

Her mouth moves, a gesture of discovery and encouragement. Lust surges through me, and I deepen the kiss, taste her fully. She tastes of spices and wine and a hint of sweetness. Better, lusher than I could have ever dreamed. And oh, have I dreamed about her.

She pulls her hands free, puts one on my chest. The curl of her fingers into my body is slight, like she wants more but is afraid to ask.

I lift her from the chair, bringing her flush against me. She's soft, warm, and smells like flowers, only better. God, I can't take it, finally letting go with her. I thrust my tongue into her mouth, my hands tightening on her arms. My instincts are racing away from my control, toward her and the need that's building in me.

I want her and she's here.

Take her, the darkest corner of my mind urges.

She shifts, her belly brushing against my cock, her breasts pressing into my chest. I can feel her nipples, high and tight, begging for my touch.

My teeth close on her lower lip. I want to devour her, to take what she's offering until we're both consumed.

She whimpers.

And I freeze.

What the fuck am I doing?

With a sharp breath, I step back and let her go. Immediately she brings a hand to her mouth, rubbing at where I've bitten her. Fuck. Fuck, fuck, fuck.

"I'm sorry." My hands curl into fists and I drop my gaze. She's a guest in my home, I've pulled her into this insane scheme, and I'm fucking mauling her here. My mother would be appalled. *I'm* appalled. "I don't know—"

I swallow the rest of that lie because I know exactly what came over me. Lust, pure and simple. I know I have to keep my fantasies at bay, to keep this all professional, and when I let loose…

"It won't happen again," I say. "I swear."

She doesn't say anything, just keeps her hand over her mouth. God, I wish I knew what she was thinking. Is she revolted? Or does she wish I'd keep going?

I grit my teeth. Actually, no, I don't want to know what she's thinking. Because if she's wishing I'd keep going, I'm in deep shit. We both are.

At least deeper shit than we're already in.

"I'll see you in the morning." I turn for the door. "We'll meet with Finn and Doc, start to sort this situation out."

I've got my fingers on the doorknob when she finally says, "I'm not sorry."

I close my eyes. That... that's exactly what I wanted her to say. But what I want isn't in this scheme. At least not what I want in the deepest, darkest part of me, the part that isn't the dutiful son, the heir to a respectable family.

I leave without acknowledging her words.

CHAPTER TEN

I can't stop running my tongue over the mark Paul left on my lower lip.

It doesn't sting anymore, not that it really did last night either. I gasped when he bit me because it was so carnal, so unlike Paul, I was shocked. But in a good way, in a "rush of heat to my pussy" kind of way.

He didn't react so well though. He acted like… like he was disgusted with himself. Which kind of killed my mood. I told him I wasn't sorry to make him feel better, to let him know everything was okay, but he didn't take it that way.

I glance up at him, sitting across the table from me. We're in the big conference room, the one they use for partner meetings. I've been in here before, but it was never just the two of us. Somehow the room feels too empty although there's not even six feet between us.

But the space is filled with fruit neither of us has touched, coffee we haven't drunk, and all the words we won't speak. He hasn't said anything to me today, at least beyond what he absolutely has to, not even during the car ride over to Bastard Capital.

When he was sneaking me out of the house this morning, I could understand the need for quiet. And on the car ride over… well, maybe he still needed to wake up. But we've got coffee now and fresh taro buns from my favorite bakery in San Francisco, so there's no more excuses.

I run my tongue over the mark one last time. He was so worked up he *bit* me. Not hard, not at all painful, but so deliciously hot and out of control.

Paul is always in control, always suave and polite. And he lost it with me.

"When will Doc and Finn get here?" I ask.

He doesn't look up from his laptop. "Soon." His cheeks darken, and I can't tell if it's because he's ashamed of his rudeness or if he's remembering last night. Or both.

"Shouldn't we be talking about our engagement?" I gesture to all the space between us. "Coming up with a more solid story about how we met, what we know about each other?"

That was why I had to be whisked to his house last night, and we've got the perfect opportunity to talk here. His mom isn't going to come bursting in. I don't think.

He sighs. "Some problems have just occurred to me about this… situation."

Meaning the kiss. I pull my mouth in tight, the better to hold in my reaction.

But then Anjie comes in, all bright and happy and looking gorgeous, and I can't tell him where he can shove his *problems.*

"Oh, I'm so happy for you two!" she gushes. "I knew something was up."

Paul stares at her. "It's fake. Just to throw off my mother. I told you that."

"You told Anjie?" I grab the arms of the chair as I sit up. "Who else?"

I thought we were supposed to be discreet here. I didn't even get a chance to tell January last night, thanks to Fuchs's message and Paul's kiss.

I wince as I imagine telling January now. Somehow, telling her it's all fake after Paul and I kissed feels like it would be lying. Although saying it's real would be lying too.

"I needed her help," Paul tells me. "And I had to tell the rest of the Bastards. It's going to look weird if they don't know we're engaged. Although they've never met my family."

"None of them?" I ask. "Not even Mark?"

Paul and Mark were friends from college—they've known each other for years. Surely somehow, somewhere, Mark should have met them. These men are practically Paul's brothers.

He shakes his head. "Of course not. Why would that ever happen?"

Wow. That's... very regimented. I'll definitely introduce January to my parents if I ever have the chance. I've certainly spoken enough about her to them.

I wonder how much of this life Paul will keep in him once he's back in Taipei. Will he still be a Bastard? Or will he cut it all away, transforming completely into the perfect heir with no trailing ends left?

Anjie clears her throat. "I meant it mostly as a joke."

"Right." Paul sends her a significant look. "Mark and Logan and Finn would say the same, of course."

I look between them, having no idea what they're talking about. What did she do to them and not to Elliott and Dev...?

"Oh no." I clap my hand over my mouth and send Anjie a horrified look. And yet...

Under my fingers, my tongue finds the tiny cut on my lip, sharp edged and bitter tasting. I can't leave it alone, not even when it hurts.

This is insanity. I'm being deported and Paul is leaving too. Anjie playing matchmaker would be ludicrous.

"Oh yes," Paul says, a warning in his tone. It's aimed at Anjie, not me though. "So no congratulations please, not even as a joke."

Anjie cuts a look at me, worry in her eyes. "All right. I'm sorry. I didn't mean to offend."

My hand is still over my mouth, and I force myself to drop it. "It's fine. I'm not offended." I smile, or try to. "It is all kind of funny, isn't it?"

But Anjie doesn't look amused. She still looks worried.

Before she can say anything, Finn comes bursting in. "I think it's hilarious," he says as he straddles a chair, the frame creaking under his weight. He looks like a professional body-builder, swollen with muscle. Or like a professional wrestler.

Doc is rolling her eyes as she comes in after him. "Ignore him. He thinks everything is a joke." Her attention turns to me. "Are you okay?"

I don't really know Doc that well; she's friends with January and works for her, but she started at January's company after I was disappeared by Corvus. I didn't get much of a chance to meet her when I was restricted to my office and my company-provided housing.

So I don't know if she's talking about my fake engagement, my immigration situation, or having been held hostage by a tech company. But I guess the answer is the same no matter what.

"I'm holding on."

We share a smile, one that says we have much more in common than we might know. I'll have to get to know Doc, at least in the few weeks I still have here.

"Good," she says, and she means it.

Finn knocks an enormous knuckle against the table. "So, Fuchs wants us to name names."

I set my shoulders, take a deep breath. "He knows he has a leak. If I tell him who it is, he'll stop obstructing my visa approval."

Doc purses her lips. "Do you actually know who it is?"

I shake my head. "Those files you were sent, the access protocol—they wouldn't be specific to one person. I mean, not everyone has them, but it's not like they're individualized."

"So like I said," Paul cuts in irritably, "give him a likely name and be done with it. He can figure it out from there."

My stomach shifts. I know that would be the easiest route and that Paul is right—I don't owe this leaker anything, and it's nothing like my great-uncle's situation—but I can't quite get it to settle inside my conscience.

"They helped us when they didn't have to," Doc points out. "I don't want Grace to lose her visa, but are we really going to sell this person out? Or someone else who may have nothing to do with it?"

Those are my thoughts exactly. Except… this leak didn't help when I was trapped inside Corvus, wondering how I was going to stop their spyware program. January and the Bastards were the ones who saved me.

"There are no innocent people working there," I say. "Including me."

It's true. We all made the choice to work for a company doing surveillance projects. We were inside the beast, and we decided to keep going, to keep doing exactly what we were doing.

"You tried to stop him," Paul says. "And you did. Twice now."

He means blocking the spyware program and using a virus to destroy the police camera surveillance program. But really, January did the first, and Doc and Finn did the second. I only helped a bit.

As if he can read my mind, Paul goes on. "Nobody would have been able to do anything about those programs if you hadn't helped. Hell, we probably still wouldn't have known about the spyware program if you hadn't smuggled that information out to January."

"Wait." Something's just occurred to me, something that

makes my skin go cold. *"I'm* the leak. I leaked that information to January."

They're all frowning at me, not understanding.

I wave my hand, indicating that I'm not done yet. "Fuchs probably knows that I passed on information about the spyware program. And he knows there's another leak, one still going on, one I can't be responsible for. So… we must be working together."

It makes so much more sense now. He's been blocking my visa not to punish me—well, yes, probably to do that too—but also to get me into this desperate situation, to give me no way out.

No way except to give up my accomplices.

I would laugh, except I have nothing to give him. Nothing except my guesses about who it could be.

"Shit," Finn breathes.

"No fucking kidding," Doc says.

Anjie spins on her heel, going for the door. "We're going to need lots more coffee."

Paul simply stares at me. There's a hardness in his gaze, as if he's not thinking of me personally but rather as a problem to be solved. I don't like it.

"What?" If he's going to keep staring like that, he can tell me what's going on in his head.

"I'm trying to think how you might use this to your advantage. If he realizes you don't know who it is, that you're scrambling because of your visa situation, it gives him the upper hand. We don't want that."

"So I lie and say I do know and that we're accomplices?" That's never going to work.

Paul shakes his head. "Not lie. But let's feel him out. See how badly he wants this name. I'm guessing he's more desperate than he's letting on. You don't have to be the one begging here."

Fuchs was my terrifying boss for so long it's hard for me

to think of him as anything else. But Paul's right—what more can Fuchs do to me beyond what he's already done? If I'm clever, I can do some demanding of my own. He came to me, not the other way around.

I'm reminded that Paul, even though he inherited his wealth, didn't coast on the luck of his birth. He's savvy, ruthless when he wants to be, and a firm ally. And an even worse enemy.

There's just one problem—I'm not really any of those things. The thought of bluffing Fuchs is giving me cold sweats. I don't know if I can pull it off.

Again, Paul reads my mind. "I'll be at the meeting with you. Don't worry, I'd never leave you alone with that monster."

Like I said, a firm ally. "Thanks" is all I can say. I don't lie and say I could have handled it myself.

Finn nods. "Good plan. But do you think you could at least come up with a few people it could have been?"

I blow out a breath, trying to remember the access protocol the mole sent them. "It definitely had to be someone at the division-manager level or above."

"How many of those are there?" Paul asks.

I shrug. "Maybe a dozen? It's hard to say because every division is so walled off from the others."

"Is it likely to be whoever was in charge of the panopticon then?" Doc asks. "Since no one else should have had access to those files."

"Possibly," I say slowly. But it doesn't entirely make sense. "The only thing is, people who get that high up at Corvus are true believers. They don't necessarily have to be great programmers at that level—they rarely touch code—but someone superloyal is more of an asset in those positions. The head of the spyware division had a tattoo of the Corvus logo, for example. She'd never betray Fuchs or the company."

Which of course made the idea of whistle-blowing that

much more terrifying. No one at Corvus would have backed me up; instead, they'd have tried their best to tear me down.

Doc drums her fingers on the table. "What about someone above the division managers then? Someone with company-wide access to the projects."

I shake my head. "That would just be Fuchs. And he's…"

My tongue slows and stops as something comes to me. Someone who's got Fuchs's kind of access, who's his right hand, his enforcer, his most trusted employee…

"It can't be her," I whisper to myself. It's crazy. She's been there for five years, has carried out his every evil directive with clear glee. She's hardly even human at this point.

"Who?" Paul demands.

I can barely say her name. It's just so inconceivable. "Minerva. She has the access, the same as Fuchs."

There's a moment of stone silence, then Finn starts laughing. I can't tell if he's amused because it's so ridiculous or if it makes perfect, crazy sense.

"No," Doc says. "She loves him. At least I think it's love."

"It has to be one of the division managers," I say. "Or someone clever enough to steal their access codes. Minerva wouldn't do that."

"But if it isn't one of the managers…," Paul says.

Then there's only one conclusion. "It has to be Minerva."

Finn's stopped laughing. Now he's thinking, his brow crinkled up. "How long has she worked for him?"

"Five years." She was there when I arrived, and I expect her to be there for a long time after this.

Doc nods. "I remember she was at Corvus back when I was working for that food-delivery-app start-up."

Paul sets his palm on the table, not forcefully, but he gets everyone's attention anyway. "It doesn't matter. The only thing that matters is getting Grace's visa settled." Just like that, he's refocused all of us. "Grace, comb through the leaked files with Finn and Doc. Once you've done that, let's ask Fuchs for a meeting. We'll plan our strategy from there."

My nerves begin to settle. Yes, I can do all that, and it feels good to have a plan, something actionable to do after all those futile job interviews. It might not work—it probably won't since Fuchs won't be satisfied with my guesses at who the mole might be—but I've got hope again.

"Sounds good," Finn says.

"I can definitely come up with some names," I say. "Beyond Minerva."

I can barely believe it might be her—Fuchs is never going to buy that suggestion.

"Oh." Paul glances upward. "I forgot—we're meeting my mother and Archie for dinner tonight."

The hope pooling in my chest goes cold. Right. I'm supposed to be playing his fiancée. I almost lost sight of the other massive complication in my life.

"Sure," I say. "The clothes got delivered this morning, so I'll be ready."

Finn and Doc share a look. Paul sees it and frowns for a moment, just a moment. Like he's not happy they're judging him.

Me too, I suppose. I agreed to this charade, and I'm in it as much as he is.

"Should we get started then?" I ask brightly. "Since I've got a date tonight."

Paul flashes me a smile of gratitude before heading for the door. He stops next to my chair and brushes my shoulder —the merest touch, probably unseen by Finn and Doc—but it shakes me down to my toes.

I let myself savor the lingering sensation for a moment, then I get to work on the files.

I've been going through these files for hours with nothing to show for it.

Paul put me in a small, unoccupied office with a desk and a computer, several flourishing snake plants in the corners and photos of wild birds in flight that are somehow soothing and energizing all at once. For a temporary office, it's very lovely.

Too bad my search of these files is not so lovely. There's no blatant sign, no flashing lights that say "Hey, here's the person that leaked all this!" Whoever it was, they were careful. And very high up at Corvus.

What's there is explosive, the choice bits from the panopticon program that give a perfect overview of the entire program. And the information about the back door into Corvus makes me gasp.

Minerva would have had access to all this. But... but there's nothing in here from outside the panopticon program. So maybe the person who sent it could only get to the panopticon files. Which wouldn't be Minerva, who has free run over everything—and if she's snapped and decided to expose Corvus, why not send everything?

It could also be someone low level who's hacked into their

boss's account. I'm assuming it has to be someone given access to the panopticon stuff, but they might have also stolen it.

I rub my forehead. This is making my head spin with too many possibilities. I need a name, just one, and there's nothing but rabbit holes here.

January popped in this morning, and I told her everything. Including about the fake engagement. She took it... not well. I think she's worried for me, although she was trying to hide it. She likes Paul, so she wasn't ready to openly criticize him. Although she was shocked.

We went through what I'd already pulled out of the files too and came up with nothing. Maybe that's why my brain keeps hopping off into speculative territory—there's nothing here to build a real case on.

My phone rings, snapping me out of my conspiracy theories. I pick it up, check the caller ID, then almost set it back down.

My parents are calling. I was supposed to call them after the Pixio interview, and I didn't. It feels like an entire lifetime has passed since then.

They'll want to know about the interview, and I'll have to admit I failed. I'll want to tell them about the engagement, but they'll be horrified. Not telling them would be the same as lying to them though.

I'm in so much trouble.

"Hello?"

"Are you getting sick? Your voice sounds creaky." My mom doesn't miss a thing.

"You should make sure your chest stays warm," Dad says. Great, they're on speakerphone together. "Are you wearing a sweater?"

They fuss over me, but it's lovely to be this loved. "I'm okay, really I am. I was working and surprised when you called. That's all."

"Are you sure?" Mom's suspicious.

"Yes, I am."

"How was the interview?" Dad asks.

I chew on my lip. "The interview went well." I'm not technically lying, because it did. "Unfortunately…"

I swallow hard and force myself to breathe. This is so hard to tell them, because they sacrificed so much to get me here. We *all* sacrificed so much for my schooling, my scholarships, applying for my visa. It wasn't just my dream—both my parents worked even harder than I did to get me where I am. I was the family project, all of us bent on my success, and I've failed.

"You can tell us," Mom says gently. She sounds like she already knows what's coming.

It's the resigned disappointment in her voice—not directed at me but at the world in general—that decides for me.

"Unfortunately," I say more firmly, "we won't hear back from Immigration Services for a while."

It's true—only the lawyers have so far said it's hopeless. Not the government themselves.

"Did you talk to the law team yesterday? Did they know how long it might take?" Dad always gets down to the practicalities.

"I didn't." Which isn't an outright lie but still feels wrong to say.

"How long do you have until the visa expires?" Mom asks. It's almost like she senses what I'm holding back and is ready to sniff out the real truth.

"Um, almost five weeks."

There's a long pause. "That seems very soon," Dad says. "I hope the paperwork can be processed in time."

Oh God. Here's where I should tell them the paperwork won't be processed in time because it will never be processed. But I don't, because I've decided that it's easier to be a bad daughter than to tell my parents the truth.

"We'll see," I say. "The lawyers are working on it."

What I'm doing now—searching within illegally obtained files for the identity of a mole—I'll never tell them about. They would be terrified for me. I also never told them about what exactly I did to get fired from Corvus. They've never asked for details, possibly because they were somewhat relieved when I was let go—the stories I told them about working there were never happy.

Another long pause. "It would be hard for Immigration Services to deny Pixio, wouldn't it?" Mom asks.

Finally I have to be brave, at least a little bit. "It's been known to happen. This isn't settled yet even if I was offered the job."

"A job offer at Pixio is a very good thing," Dad says bracingly, finding the small bit of luck in all this. "You would be privileged to work there."

"I would," I agree solemnly. Too bad it won't happen.

Mom sighs. "What have you been doing besides preparing for your interview? Have you been eating properly? What did you cook this week?"

"I cooked some soup. Chicken was on sale." My stomach unknots as we move into more ordinary things. I should be able to keep them talking about food, how well I've been sleeping, and my general health until they hang up.

"Good," Mom says. She believes cooking for yourself at home at least once a week is the way to keep in good health. If she knew how much I ate out—and American food at that —she'd faint from shock.

Dad clears his throat. "Has Mr. Tsai said anything?"

I go very still. My parents know that Paul is helping me, but to them he's some far-off figure, too famous to really be helping their daughter. They almost never mention him when I call, but they ask a lot about the lawyers and what they have to say.

"Mr. Tsai arranged for the interview at Pixio," I say. "He… he has many contacts within the government here."

"He talked to them for you?" Mom asks cautiously.

"He did." I don't elaborate on what those contacts told him. "He's been very kind."

"Of course," Mom says. "To arrange for the lawyers, to speak to the officials. We can never repay him."

No, we can't. And she says we because keeping me in America is a family effort. If I get a green card, it would be a triumph for all three of us.

Dad hums deep in his throat, the noise he makes when he's not certain of something. Or when he hears something he believes to be untrue but can't outright speak against it. "You've also worked very hard to be worthy of the opportunities Mr. Tsai is providing," he says to me. "Don't forget that."

He means that I shouldn't give all the credit to Paul—but I must also keep striving and not rely on Paul's favors too much. Because someday they will not be there.

Before I can respond, Paul opens the office door and pokes his head in. "Hi. Just seeing how you're doing. Do you want any lunch?" He smiles sheepishly. "Well, Anjie is ordering lunch, so whether you want it or not, some is coming. She doesn't take no for an answer very well."

My phone is on speaker. My parents heard every word.

"Who is that?" Mom asks.

"It's Mr. Tsai," I say. *My parents*, I mouth at Paul.

"Ah," he says softly. And comes into the room.

I'm blinking madly at him when my mother says, "He's there? With you?"

I jerk at my throat, making a slashing motion. *Shut up, disappear, don't give away a thing* are all notions I'm trying to get across with that one motion.

"A pleasure to speak with you, Mr. and Mrs. Li," he says, all golden, perfect manners. Of course he has to be polite and not simply disappear.

"We thank you for everything you've done for Grace," Mom says. There's a delighted flutter in her voice.

Dad says nothing. I don't think Paul's won him over like he has Mom.

"It was nothing." Paul looks right into my eyes as he says it. "Of course we must keep Grace here. She's worked so hard for the opportunity."

Mom laughs softly. "She has. I'm glad you appreciate that." She's preening because Paul is complimenting all of us even if he doesn't know it.

Or maybe he does. Certainly he understands the deep ties of family.

"We'll call again tomorrow," Dad says. "You should get back to work now."

He never asked me exactly what I'm working on. He simply trusts that I'm doing something important and should get back to it. That kind of trust is a blessing, and I'm abusing it.

But if I can resolve my visa issues, it will all be worth it.

"Okay," I say, my finger hovering over the End Call button.

"Keep warm and eat properly," Mom warns.

"I'll make sure of it," Paul says.

Before this call can get any worse, I say "Bye" as quickly as I can, then end the call. But I'm still flushed all over from the way Paul said that. Like he was pretending for my parents that we're really engaged.

"They don't know," I say so that he understands. "All they know is that I was fired and I'm trying to get a new job. And that you're helping with the job search and paying for the lawyers. Not about the engagement."

He raises an eyebrow. "You're lying to your parents?"

I simply stare at him. That's really something coming from him.

"I mean," he says, "you don't seem like the kind of person to do that."

"I'm not." I stare at the phone, which is dark. "But circumstances are extreme at the moment. If I can get this visa without them knowing about everything else happening… They don't need the stress. They've already done so much to get me here."

After what happened to my uncle, my father deserves some ease. Deserves to have his daughter be happy and secure in the life he wanted for her. It's the least I can give him.

Paul nods. "I understand. Family is…" He smiles and lifts his hands in a gesture that says everything he can't.

"Exactly."

Our eyes lock and we share a moment of sympathy and understanding. And after a heartbeat, it sparks into something more.

Then we both blink and the moment's gone. "I'll bring you some lunch," Paul says.

I should protest, tell him he doesn't have to, I can get it myself. But I kind of like the idea of him waiting on me. "Thank you."

"My pleasure." His voice vibrates and skips through all the sensitive parts of me.

And when he leaves, I can't stop running my tongue over the mark he left on my lip.

CHAPTER TWELVE

All the Bastards are assembled in the conference room, and they're looking at me funny.

I can't tell if it's because I've called a partners' meeting out of the blue or if it's because they heard about my engagement. Probably both.

"I'm still not sure if I'm supposed to congratulate you or not," Mark says. "January wasn't clear on that."

Grace and January have probably been talking all morning about… everything. I'm not sure how much of what they talked about got back to Mark, but clearly it was enough to confuse him.

"Thanks, but there's no need for congratulations."

The entire room goes silent at that. I realize that while they've always been on my side, faking an engagement with an innocent woman might be a bridge too far for even them.

"She agreed," I say hastily. "It's all completely impersonal."

Except for that kiss last night. That was deeply, deeply personal. Hell, I'm getting hot just remembering it.

"So…" Logan tilts his head, confused. "Congratulations? I don't get it."

Logan is happily married—although he wasn't for a while —and he's been disgustingly sappy since he and Callie reconciled and she got pregnant. He's not going to be enthused about faking an engagement.

I sigh. Explaining my family to them isn't going to be easy. "It's complicated."

Although Grace understood almost immediately. Yeah, she protested at first and wasn't entirely happy about learning all my cousins' names, but in the end, she got it. Explaining things to her was never a chore.

"I really hope you're not fucking with Grace," Mark says wearily. "January will lose it if you are, and I'll have to fight you."

I roll my eyes. I might not have the muscle mass of Mark, but I guarantee I've got him beat in hand-to-hand combat, especially when I attend grappling sessions weekly. "Yeah, I'm really scared. And no, I'm not fucking with Grace. We're only pretending to be engaged, and we're both on the same page."

But what page might that be now? The one we meant to start and stay on or the one that includes kissing? And other things?

These are not questions I can or want to answer.

Finn looks like I told them I've decided to walk backward for the rest of my life. "Why would you do that?"

"Because my mother decided I needed to get married and even picked out the girl for me." I keep my tone carefully free of any judgment on my mother. I can be mad at her about it, but no one else can. I mean, she's still my mother.

Logan's jaw drops. "That's, uh, that's kind of extreme." I get the sense he wants to use a different word, one closer to crazy. He clears his throat when I don't respond. "Of course, she's your mom, and I'm sure the girl is nice—"

"I don't know if I'd call her nice," I say as I recall Amelia's expression and demeanor when she was talking to Grace at the restaurant the other night. No, she hadn't looked nice then.

Maybe Lucy is right about Amelia. Thank God I'm not going to marry her.

I focus back on Logan. "But my mother thinks she's suitable."

Finn bursts out laughing. "Suitable? Like you're a duke or something?"

It does sound pretty ridiculous when he puts it like that. Except I do need to find a suitable wife to help me manage my family. I can't marry just anyone.

I shrug. "I had to think fast, with my mother announcing she'd brought Amelia with her and I ought to propose soon. Grace happened to be right there and went along with it. But none of it is real. We're faking it."

"I'm sure *she* is," Finn says with a wicked grin.

I'm tempted to kick his shin under the table, but I hold back. "I'm sure you have a lot of experience with that."

Finn snorts. "You're projecting, dude."

I have to stop and catch my breath before I can go on, because I'm going to miss this. The banter, the jokes, having five almost brothers who love me and tease me in equal measures. I'd never give up my family back home, but finding a family like this—one we made ourselves—was something I never expected when I moved here.

God, now I'm getting as sappy as Logan.

"I'm not going to say any more because I respect Doc too much." I try to look noble. It's a weak response, but I was too busy getting choked up to come up with anything better.

Finn rolls his eyes, but there's a hint of concern in his expression. Like he knows I almost lost it.

Telling them all I'm leaving soon is going to be harder than I imagined.

"Are you actually going to marry her?" asks Dev.

Everyone gets quiet. It's a strange question from him, especially since he's the loner among us. We're all close, but I sometimes get the sense Dev would be perfectly fine if we all disappeared tomorrow.

"No," I say quietly. "She's not staying here. And neither am I. I need to go back to Taipei."

I can tell from their expressions they don't understand, that they think it will be a short trip.

"For how long?" Elliott asks. "Because we're still in the middle of the SciCorp deal."

"Probably kind of forever," I say, keeping my tone level even as my throat tightens.

The only response to that is a shocked silence. Then they all start talking at once. It's mostly denials and yells of "bull-shit" and "what the fuck" and "why are you leaving," and all of it warms my heart, strangely enough.

I came to America to get a break from my family. To be something besides Lillian's son and the heir to everything. To get away from always being perfect and responsible and worthy of my title. These guys became a second family to me and let me be something entirely different. I'm going to miss it. Way more than I expected.

But it's not like I'm dying here.

"I'm not giving up my partnership," I say, motioning for them to quiet down. "I can work remotely from Taipei; it's not a big deal. I'm not abandoning you."

"But why?" Mark asks. "Why do you have to leave the Bay Area then?"

"My mother wants to retire," I say simply. "I can't tell her no."

Finn visibly softens. "Ah, man, your mom. If you gotta do it for her…"

"Yeah," Logan says gruffly. "If your mom needs you, then she needs you."

I clear my throat, harder this time. I'm definitely not going to cry, not a chance, but my chest is kind of tight. And my eyes burn, a little. Just a little.

"I figured you guys would understand," I say, forcing my voice down low so it doesn't break. "We all knew I'd have to take over the family business someday."

I knew, of course, have known my entire life, but facing it—leaving my life in America behind—is tough. Even knowing that this was coming isn't making it any easier.

"Of course we understand. But we'll miss your beautiful face," Mark says with a grin.

"And your connections." Logan makes that a blunt joke.

Elliott moves then, and I suddenly realize how still he's been this entire time. "And where does that leave Grace?"

Grace. Somehow her name has become a touchstone to me, something I have to internally echo each time I hear it. "I'm giving her a very generous amount of money after this, enough for her to do whatever she wants, even in Beijing." I adjust my cuffs even though they're mostly fine. "We've run out of options with Immigration. So this is the next best thing."

Then why do I feel like such a shit bag about it? Grace is smart, savvy—I didn't force her into anything. I really did try everything with her visa situation. I'm the fucking nice one around here, the least bastardly of the Bastards. I shouldn't be feeling like this. I *never* feel like this.

"What about the Fuchs thing?" Finn asks. "Did Grace figure out who the mole was?"

I realize then I have to explain to all of them—except for Finn—about the whole Fuchs thing. "Fuchs contacted Grace, told her he'd fix her visa problems if she'd tell him who leaked all that stuff to Doc and Finn," I say quickly to everyone. "No"—I look at Finn—"she hasn't. We're supposed to meet with him tomorrow, feel him out."

"That's really generous of him," Elliott says coldly, "considering he's the source of all her visa problems."

I nod tiredly. "Yeah, well, he's kind of an asshole if you hadn't noticed. Anyway, if she can give him some names and get him to drop his bullshit, that problem's solved. But she doesn't know exactly who it could be."

Finn taps his knuckles against the table. "She did suggest Minerva."

Elliott laughs at that, a nasty, ugly noise. "Right, because Minerva's definitely going to turn against her lord and master. Fuck, she worships that asshole. Did you see how she gets off on carrying out his orders, ruining people's lives when he tells her to?"

None of us like Minerva, but with Elliott it's deeper. It's almost like he can't forgive her for her role in Fuchs's schemes. Fuchs he can understand at least—the dude's a certified sociopath and there's no reasoning with that—but Minerva at least still seems human, somewhat. Maybe it's her sadism, cold, clinical, that really hits at Elliott.

Dev takes a deep breath, steepling his fingers. "It's interesting that Fuchs—notorious for the control he has over his employees' lives—seems to have no idea what's happening within one of his most secure divisions."

"Interesting and a definite show of weakness," I say. "He wouldn't have come to Grace if he wasn't desperate and in the dark. That gives her leverage."

Dev stares off at nothing for a moment, then suddenly rises. "I have to make some calls." He leaves without another word.

We all stare after him, because what the fuck was that?

"Is anyone noticing that he's getting…" Logan cocks his head as he searches for the right word.

"More secretive?" I supply.

"Colder?" Mark offers.

"Weirder?" Finn suggests.

Elliott frowns at the door Dev just shut behind him. "I haven't noticed anything."

Logan sighs in that older sibling way, the one I use with

Lucy all the time. "Dude." The word drips with exasperation and resignation.

"What?" Elliott's offended now.

"Look, as great as this has been"—I shoot back my cuff to check my watch—"I need to get ready for dinner tonight. Hopefully Fuchs will somehow spill everything tomorrow during our meeting and clear all this confusion up for us, just like a villain monologueing in the last act."

"Good luck," Logan says. "With everything."

"Punch Fuchs in the balls for me," Mark says cheerily. "And say hi to Grace."

I grab my jacket from the back of my chair. "I can definitely do one of those."

"Man, Grace is gonna be so pissed when you don't say hi to her," Finn deadpans.

I sling my jacket over my shoulder and head for the door. I could stay here and trade insults all day, but I've got to go see my fake fiancée and tell her hi. Strangely, I've kind of missed her today, even after seeing her at lunch and talking with her parents.

And as enjoyable as punching Fuchs in the balls would be, I'd much rather greet Grace at the end of the day.

CHAPTER THIRTEEN

It turns out that the "small dining room" is actually bigger than my entire apartment. My old one, not the one Paul is letting me live in.

"It'll just be a simple dinner," Paul had said. "In the small dining room."

I should have known that the small dining room in a house like Paul's would be like something out of the Forbidden Palace. There's a chandelier and a massive walnut table and servants refilling our glasses and plates before we've even noticed they're low. It's an intimate luxury, but a luxury nonetheless.

While this dinner is more intimate than the large, loud gathering last night—it's me, Paul, his mother, Lucy, and Archie and his wife—the currents of family dynamics I'm swimming through are just as complex. Maybe even more so.

For example, why is Archie here? He's not part of the immediate family, and I can tell that Lillian—thinking of her by that name is odd, but I can't call her "Paul's mom" all the time—doesn't particularly like him. She hides it well, but there's the faintest curl to her lip, a tightness at the edges of her mouth, each time he speaks.

Mostly he's been talking about business deals and ideas

for investments. I can't tell if he's trying to impress Lillian or Paul or if he's simply making the case that he should have inherited control rather than Paul. I don't know enough about real estate in Hong Kong to say if his ideas are good or not, but I can tell that Paul's had enough of it by the time the fish is served.

I take up the serving fork when the maid comes in, the fish still steaming with heat, offering the fish cheeks to Lillian. She takes them with a brief expression of thanks.

"Tell us," I say to her, ignoring Archie's attempt to keep going about another deal, "how has your trip been so far?"

Archie has to stop talking unless he wants to insult me. And if Lillian answers, he'll be insulting her. And if he insults me, he'll be insulting Paul too. I'm just trying to defuse the tension in the room, but I'm also realizing that as Paul's fiancée, I have a strange kind of social power.

And if I've violated any unspoken rules by speaking over Archie, they can excuse it due to my mainland upbringing.

"It's been cold," Lillian says, disapproval in her tone. I can't tell if she's disappointed in the weather or me, as if I should have done something personally about the cold snap the area's been having. She sniffs, then takes a bite of fish cheek.

I catch Paul's eye from the corner of my gaze, and he's got a half smile of approval. He quirks his eyebrows once, quickly, when our gazes meet. *Thanks for shutting Archie up,* his expression says.

"You came at a bad time," Paul says mildly. At his mother's sharp look, he adds, "Weather-wise."

"Does your apartment have heat?" she asks me out of the blue. Her expression is so intense I know she's not asking out of any concern for my comfort.

"Um, yes." My cheeks flush as I remember exactly who owns the apartment where I'm supposed to be staying. And who owns the house where I slept last night. If she asks where I live, she might be able to figure out her family owns the building I'm in. That wouldn't be as bad as her knowing I'm staying in Paul's house, but it wouldn't be good.

"Were you warm enough last night? Because I wasn't."

My mouth almost drops open when she says that. Because… does she actually suspect we stayed under the same roof last night? Is that what she's getting at?

Lillian Tsai didn't make her money by being a fool, but I'm starting to suspect she's more cunning than I ever dreamed.

I plaster on an apologetic smile. "Paul, turn up the heat for your mother. That's what I did last night," I say to her. "I turned up the thermostat. In my apartment."

She must hear the emphasis I put on *my*, but she doesn't react. She makes a noise acknowledging that she heard me, but she's not going to continue the conversation.

"Mother, that wing has its own AC and heater and climate control," Paul says. "If you were cold, you could have done something about it."

I can't tell if Paul suspects what his mother is up to with her line of questions. Or if maybe she's a touch eccentric and I'm too paranoid about it.

I serve the fish to the rest of the table, saving Lucy for last. "You're doing great," she whispers to me as I lean over her plate.

"It doesn't feel great," I whisper back. Mostly I've been quiet while Archie has lectured us. I don't know that my redirection of the conversation was that successful in the end.

After I serve myself, I sit back down. There's a lull in the conversation as everyone starts their fish, and luckily Archie doesn't seem inclined to fill the silence.

Underneath the table, Paul brushes my thigh. He doesn't look at me as he does it, and I'm guessing he meant it as a gesture of support, but my lips throb anyway when he does it. I've never been so achingly aware of another person, another body, and my own at the same time.

He reaches for his wineglass, his fingers elegant but strong, and my own fingers tingle. His throat works as he swallows, and my own throat tightens. His shirt pulls against his shoulders, his body straining the fabric, and my own skin strains to touch his.

The moment lasts less than two heartbeats, but it turns something in me around, an awareness that completely, fully focuses on Paul and can't be budged.

"We'll go shopping later this week," Lucy says to me, and I force myself to breathe, to pay attention to her. "The sooner you choose a dress, the sooner the alterations can be done. Really, we're cutting it very close."

She's leaped too far ahead for me. Surely she can't mean a wedding gown?

Oh, but Paul would look devastating in a tux, waiting at the front of a church, the Bastards assembled next to him, his hands clasped and a small smile on his face as he waits for his bride. The image is almost painfully romantic.

His knee brushes mine, entirely by accident I think, and my heart sighs.

"Um, what for?" I ask Lucy, telling my silly body and brain to calm the eff down. I'm supposed to be pretending here, not fantasizing.

"The gala." She laughs like she finds me too silly for words. I have to smile because she has a compelling laugh. "You'll need a gown. I ordered mine months ago—they're flying it in next week. Or at least they should be. Oh, Paul, I'm going to need the plane that week."

She's going to use her family's private jet to fly in a dress. Right. Of course. "Where… where did you get the dress?"

I already know it's going to be Paris or Milan or some European city so trendy I don't even know it's trendy yet. Maybe Kiev's designers have upped their game.

"From Henri Zidane." Lucy tosses that off like they're old friends. I don't recognize the name, but I'm sure if I picked up the latest copy of *Vogue*, I'd see him in there. "He's still deciding what to do now that he's left Chanel. I keep telling him, 'Start your own house!' but he wants to revive some old luxury name. It's a dream of his."

I nod as if that's a perfectly reasonable dream to have, that all my schoolmates dreamed the same thing.

Archie's wife sees her opportunity. "How lovely that he agreed to do it. I was just telling Aja—he took over from Henri," she says to me, "that I so hope Henri lands on his feet."

Lucy tilts her head. "Is Aja doing your gown?"

"Of course." Archie's wife laughs, but it's nowhere near as charming as Lucy's. "That's why I was talking with him." She turns to me. "I'm sure you'll find something perfectly... *adequate* off the rack."

It's clear she intends that to be deeply wounding, but I'm mostly amused. Whatever off-the-rack gown Lucy finds for me is going to be the most expensive item of clothing I've ever worn, and I'm perfectly fine with that. "I'm sure I'll find something I love," I say. "I'm not picky. For a programmer, buying new sneakers is considered dressing up."

That seems to catch his mother by surprise. "You're a programmer? You make software?"

I nod. *I'm not just your son's fake fiancée.* "I've been working in tech since I graduated university. Or before, actually—I got my first job as a coder the summer I turned sixteen."

His mother looks impressed by my work ethic, which is why I mentioned it. I wonder nastily for a moment if Amelia has ever had a job in her life. Probably not. And then I feel guilty even though Amelia doesn't need my sympathy.

"What exactly are you doing now?" Lillian asks.

I know better than to detail my long, sad story with Corvus and my current unemployment status. She probably already suspects I'm marrying Paul for his money—no need to have her thinking I'm marrying him for a green card too.

Not that I'm going to marry him at all. *Remember?*

"I'm doing some security work," I say, which is true. Combing through the leaked files to find the mole is security related. "Mostly involving encryption." Again true, although the code I'm trying to break is a person's identity rather than a secret message.

His mother sits back, her mouth pursing. "Interesting. That's a rapidly growing market back home. I've been considering several options recently in that field."

Meaning China is looking to spy harder on its citizens and clamp down on even more information within the country, and several tech companies want to make some money off that. My hands aren't clean—they never could be since I worked at Corvus—but I still shudder inside. "I imagine you could get a very nice return on your investment with some of those companies," I say carefully. "But you'd have to consider who you'd be doing business with."

Meaning a government that represses its own people, one that doesn't even consider her country to be independent. To China, Taiwan is a naughty child that will one day get the thrashing it so richly deserves.

I don't think Lillian Tsai views her home like that though.

She nods slowly, wisely. "True. We want to invest with an eye for centuries rather than months. It's the only way the family will endure." She shifts, subtly, and suddenly seems older, smaller. "But it will be Paul's responsibility from now on."

Paul meets his mother's gaze, and he transforms too, his jaw squaring, his chest lifting. He's turning from a prince into a king, right before my very eyes. "You have nothing to worry about. I know my duty."

It's such a lovely moment, my eyes start to water. Lucy's mouth is wobbling and she's blinking, affected by it too.

And then Archie opens his mouth and ruins it. "We'll be here to help him too."

Paul looks right at me and rolls his eyes. He doesn't look at his mother or even his sister—he looks at me, shares that emotion with me.

I smile very sweetly at Paul while addressing Archie. "I know Paul is so relieved to hear that." I'm amazed at how sincere I sound.

Archie is convinced by my act—I can tell by the contempt at the edges of his smile. *You silly girl*, that expression says. "And he'll have you."

"Which I'm very grateful for," Paul says without missing a beat, taking my hand and running his thumb over my knuckles. The gesture is both possessive and cherishing. I have to forcefully remind myself that it's fake as hell too.

"How did you two meet?" Archie asks, like he's expecting a supercute, superromantic story. But his eyes are sharp.

Paul looks at me, his expression fond, as if he's waiting for me to begin a story that's all too familiar to him.

"I'm good friends with January Harris," I explain. "She's dating Mark, Paul's partner."

No recognition flashes across their faces, and I remember that they've never met Mark. I wonder exactly how much about his partners Paul's told his family. I'm guessing not much.

"Mark Taylor," I clarify. "At... From their venture capital firm."

I was just about to say Bastard Capital when I caught myself in time. I can't say a word that rude to his mother even if it is the name of the place where her son is a partner.

"There's more to it than that," Paul says. "You're leaving out all the good bits."

Meaning all the details we so carefully worked out together, the ones that were supposed to make our story more believable.

"Like what?" Lucy demands. She looks between us, and I can tell she wants Paul to pick up some slack and do some telling himself.

Thank goodness for little sisters who aren't impressed by their brothers.

"There was a get-together at the office." Paul watches me as he speaks. "We'd just finished a very intense, very tricky project, and January and Grace came to celebrate with us."

"I didn't know about this project," Lillian says. "What was it? Was the deal announced in the financial papers?"

Paul shakes his head. "It was a few months ago. Very secret. We were worried it would never happen, that we'd fail." He takes a moment, remembering, but since he's making all this up, I don't know what he could be recalling. "But we didn't, and it was such a triumph and a relief, and then there was Grace."

Oh. *Oh.* He *is* remembering something real, but it wasn't a few months ago, it was a few weeks ago. Almost five, actually.

He's talking about when they got me out of Corvus. That's the very first time I met him, saw him. Rescuing me was the thing they were worried wouldn't happen.

I was horribly shaken up that night, but I still remember Paul, how struck I was by his presence. And he's pretending here that he was as impressed by that moment as I was.

"It was quite an accomplishment," I say. "And I'm glad I was there to celebrate."

We share a brief, secret smile at my little joke.

"January wanted me to meet Mark," I say. Which is a lie, because I had no idea at the time who Mark was. I was cut off from everything by Corvus. "So she dragged me along. Mark was nice, of course, but Paul…"

I let that hang, allowing them to imagine everything I was feeling that I'm too shy to confess out loud.

"You knew who he was," his mother says flatly. Meaning, I knew he was *the* Paul Tsai.

It might look better if I say I didn't—look at how innocent I am; I've never read a gossip site in my life—but that would probably be a lie too far.

"Yes," I say.

"But she didn't care," Paul says. His voice has dropped a few notes. "It took a few times before she'd agree to go on a date."

Archie rears back in surprise. "You said no? To him?" He actually points at Paul, like he can't believe I'd ever do it.

"I did. I was very busy at work," I say primly.

Lucy tucks her chin in her hand, smiling as if I really did turn her brother down. His mother raises an eyebrow but says nothing.

"How many times did she say no?" Lucy asks. "I want exact numbers."

Paul and I laugh together. This isn't the story we rehearsed before, but we're spinning something new. It's all lies, but it feels magical. Like we're really building something.

He looks at me. "How many times was it? My heart was too bruised after the first rejection to keep track."

"Hmm." I pretend to count on my fingers. "Four that night, at least. But I took pity on you once you started texting me."

"Pity?" Lillian sits up straight.

Oops. I guess I'm not supposed to use that word in conjunction with her golden child.

"Yes, Mom," Lucy says. "Pity. I mean, look at him. I feel sorry for him."

Lillian looks at her son, beams at him really, then shakes her head wryly. I realize that Lucy can get away with things with her mother that Paul can't or maybe doesn't even try. Just as the family needs Paul to be the heir, the responsible one, they need Lucy to be the funny, irreverent one.

Which makes me wonder—what do they need from Paul's wife? I suppose she should photograph beautifully in her designer gowns, know everyone in their social circle, raise their children well. Amelia would fit all those criteria.

But… but I think they need someone more than just that. Someone who can fill a bigger role.

I wonder if Paul realizes that subconsciously, which is why he rejected Amelia.

But I also know it's not my concern. This thing between us is fake, and he'll make something real, true, with his wife. Besides, even if I can't quite define it, I know I'm not the woman to fill that bigger role no matter how well I'm pretending. Because it *is* all pretend.

And that kiss? my inner voice asks slyly. *That felt pretty real. Almost as real as all this.*

"Don't feel sorry for me." Paul squeezes my hand, which he's been holding this entire time. "She said yes in the end."

The look he sends me is so dazzling I have to look away before I give us both away by crying.

CHAPTER FOURTEEN

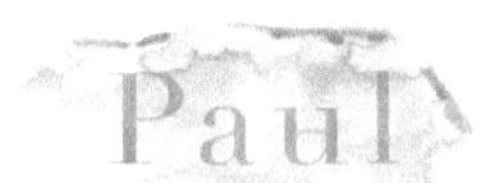

"He's purposefully late," I growl as I hand Grace a paper bag with a pastry inside. "Fuchs is never late, so he's fucking with us."

The wind is strong today, cold and wild as it whips through the gardens and along the façade of Saint Patrick's, stony and sturdy. Grace's hair keeps falling into her face, and she tries to push the bag away. "I'm too nervous to eat."

I wrap her hands around it. "You have to. You have to seem casual, like you hold all the cards. If you're eating and he's not, then you don't care as much as he does."

"Does he eat?" she mutters, pulling off a small piece of croissant.

"Only small children."

She smiles, which is exactly what I wanted her to do. The more relaxed she is, the easier it will be to feel Fuchs out. He's not going to give anything away if he senses even a hint of weakness in Grace. He respects strength, bows down to it. So she's going to have to be strong as fuck.

Which... I'm beginning to suspect she already is. She sailed through dinner last night, charming Lucy, impressing my mother, and even holding off Archie's bloviating. I'm pretty sure she's got this.

I have to admit I was impressed by her last night too. And charmed. And aroused. I had to hold her hand, to make it look real, but once I touched her, I couldn't let go. Her skin was soft enough to shove my imagination into overdrive, picturing all the places on her body where her skin would be even softer and thinking how much I'd like to explore those places with my mouth.

Like her lips. I already knew those were pretty damn soft. Soft enough to get my cock hard in an instant.

"Want some?" Grace blinks up at me, the afternoon sun bright on her face as she offers me a bite of croissant.

I do want some, but not what she's got in her hand. "No. I'm fine."

"Shouldn't you seem casual too? You look… anxious."

I am, but I'll get myself under control once he arrives. "I'm your muscle. I'm not casual, I'm mean."

She giggles. "Right."

And then she stops, her tongue darting out to wet her bottom lip. She pauses over a particular spot, tasting it again and again.

I run my tongue over my teeth, remembering how fucking hot it was to bite that pretty mouth of hers. Not hard, not mean, but just enough to let her know I meant it.

Nope. I put the heels of my hands into my eyes. I'm not going down this path. Although I was highly tempted, I managed to keep far away from her room last night. I mean, I paced the floor, thinking about what she might do if I did come knocking and how quickly I could get her naked, but I didn't do it. I'm not an animal.

But God, do I want to get primitive with her.

"Don't worry about me." My tone is snappier than I wanted, probably because I'm mostly pissed at myself. "Eat your croissant."

Her mood deflates, and I feel like an ass. She listlessly puts a piece in her mouth, chews like it's sawdust.

Fuck. I should apologize. But before I can, she stiffens.

"He's here."

I turn to see. Sure enough, Fuchs is stepping out of a double-parked black sedan, ignoring all the traffic honking behind him.

I wait, watch. No one else seems to be in the car besides the driver. He's come alone.

Which means... he might suspect Minerva. I can't remember a time when she wasn't at Fuchs's side, even when he was doing the most illegal, immoral shit.

"The mole. It's her. Minerva," I whisper to Grace.

"Are you sure?"

"Give him her name." I have no right to order her, but I do it anyway. She gives Fuchs that one little name and her problems are over.

Grace will be able to stay. The thought makes me happier than any I've had in a long time. And all Grace has to do is point the finger at someone who more than deserves it.

But Fuchs isn't shutting the car door. He's out, but he's waiting, holding it open.

Two long legs appear, wearing black wool trousers. Then Minerva herself is there, in a severely cut black suit with a dark gray top under, and she's got black leather gloves on. The outfit is almost cartoonishly evil-looking, which was probably what Minerva was going for.

Fuchs offers her a hand as she exits, and she takes it with an expression of purest gratitude. It hurts to see because she looks like she's desperately in love with him and knows he'll never, ever love her back. But she'll take what she can get.

There goes my brilliant theory.

There's no time to tell Grace that—Fuchs and Minerva are coming toward us and we need to put our game faces on. Thank God we've already gotten practice in lying together.

"Arne." I say his name as if this meeting is some happy surprise, and I hold out my hand. "How are you?"

He ignores me. "Who is it?" He launches that demand at Grace. "Tell me now. You're making me angry with this delay."

I step between them, my cool entirely gone. "You need to change your tone, *fucking immediately,* or we're out of here."

Fuchs blinks at me like he's just now realized I'm here. There's sweat on his forehead, his skin is pasty, and there're bags under his eyes. He looks like he's got food poisoning and the flu all at once.

Somebody's good and riled about his little leak. Excellent.

He takes a step back. I don't back off.

He takes another step away, then another. I let myself relax.

"I don't understand," he says. "Why are you here?"

"We're engaged," I say. "Thanks for the good wishes."

Behind me, Grace makes a noise that might be a stifled laugh.

Fuchs looks between us while Minerva stares on impassively.

"Do you have the name?" This time his tone is much nicer to Grace. Or at least not as hostile.

"I need guarantees before I'll give it to you," she says, cool as anything. "You understand why I can't simply trust your word."

"There's nothing to give." His voice is flat, but underneath there's a vibration of fury. "You give me your accomplice and I get your visa approved."

"So you are the one blocking her visa?" I ask.

He's mad, but not quite mad enough to get caught by that. "The name. I want it."

"And I want my visa approved first." Grace crosses her arms, looking so badass I can't help but stare. "That's my final offer."

Fuchs sets his jaw, watching her. I watch Minerva, trying to see if she's feeling anything at all beyond bored competence. But her expression looks the same as it always does.

Her boss, on the other hand, is going through some stuff. Mostly rage. "You don't get to bargain with me," he says. "Tell me their name."

"Or what?" Grace isn't fierce—she's too controlled for that—but there's a new kind of power running through her. "You can't control me anymore. You fired me, blocked my visa. What will you do next, kill me?"

Even Fuchs flinches at that. Minerva, surprisingly, doesn't.

"I didn't think so," Grace says, as cool as ever. "I've got nothing left to lose. You've taken everything you thought you could. But I'm not beaten. You want that name? Give me my visa."

She's like an empress, demanding her defeated foe bend the knee. I don't think it's working on Fuchs—he looks as angry as ever—but it's still fucking impressive.

"I'll find your little gang without you," he says. "And I'll make them pay. You too—an international border is nothing to me. Do you know how much business I do with the Chinese government? You're nothing to them compared to that."

Heated rage runs through me. "Do you know how much business I do with the Chinese government?" I ask. "There's no way you'll be touching my wife."

A jolt runs between Grace and me as we both suddenly realize that I'm lying. But it was such an instinctive response —to claim her as mine felt so right.

She blinks at me, her mouth parting, and then she tilts her chin, subtly pointing at Fuchs.

Right. He's just given away that he thinks she's working with someone still inside Corvus. So he doesn't really know much about his leak at all. I'm not sure how we can use that information, but it's good to have.

However, Fuchs isn't completely stupid—he tilts his head, studying the two of us, sensing that something's off. "Why are you here then? You don't need a visa, not if you're marrying him."

"Because I want what's mine," Grace says. "I worked hard for that visa, harder than you'll ever imagine. And I want it."

That's something Fuchs can understand, that pure, grasping greediness. *Mine. Give it to me.*

But he thinks Grace owes him that name, that it rightfully belongs to him, so he's going to hold on to the only leverage he's got on her. I can already see it.

He turns on his heel. "I want all your conspirators first. And when it checks out—and I prosecute all of them to the fullest extent of the law—only then will you get your visa." The ice in his voice makes a chill run down my spine. I'm not afraid for myself, but when he finds the person he's looking for…

My gaze swings over to Minerva, who's barely moved this entire time. If she is the mole, then she's got guts of pure steel, because she hasn't blinked once. We're sitting here, discussing finding, exposing, and punishing her, and she's as calm, as robotic as ever.

She and Fuchs definitely deserve each other.

Fuchs looks at me, then shakes his head. "I thought you'd choose someone smarter to marry." He says it like he's offering me serious advice.

I see red for a moment, then force myself to calm down. Finn would have laid him out for that, and Mark and Logan probably would have too, but there are more elegant ways to fight. Although no less deadly.

"She was smart enough to tell you off," I say with a razor smile. "Oh, and I'll be chatting with Arthur Wu this week. He's an old friend of mine." Arthur is also one of the most powerful men in Singapore. Nothing gets done in that business community without Arthur's say-so, including the very lucrative surveillance and security contract with the government. "You know Arthur, don't you?"

Of course Fuchs does—he would have had to kiss Arthur's ass in order to do business in Singapore. And I know Corvus does a lot of business in Singapore. But not once I'm done talking with Arthur.

Fuchs gives me a piercing look but says nothing.

"Good luck in your search," Grace says, bored as she dismisses him.

He stomps off then, toward his car which is still double-parked, Minerva following behind.

We watch until the car pulls away, both of us processing it all.

"What just happened?" Grace asks.

"You told Arne Fuchs to go fuck himself, only much more elegantly."

"I guess I did." She sounds kind of dreamy, like she can't quite believe that was her.

But it was. She was magnificent. I start to tell her that, then catch myself.

I told Arne Fuchs she was going to be my wife. Hell, I practically planted an electric fence around her and dared him to touch. And it felt amazing. And most frightening of all, real.

It can't feel real. That was the deal.

CHAPTER FIFTEEN

I'm not sure if I'm shaking because I'm cold or because I just told Arne Fuchs to go to hell.

Paul pulled me into a coffee shop around the corner when I started shivering. I've got a cup of tea between my hands—a blend that smells lovely, because of course Paul would get lovely tea—and the shop is warm, but I can't stop my teeth from chattering. It's like the bitter wind outside is stuck inside me.

Paul is watching me with a grim expression. He's probably appalled by my reaction since I was pretending to be so brave earlier. But I can't seem to get ahold of myself.

"Sorry," I say through my clenched teeth. It comes out jagged. "I can't—"

He sighs loudly enough to cut me off, takes my mug away, then takes my hands between his. "I shouldn't have let you do this."

I shake my head. "You couldn't have stopped me." Strangely, my hands are feeling warmer. Almost hot. And that heat is seeping into the rest of me, chasing away the shivers.

Paul rubs my fingers between his palms. My heart sparks at the gesture. "I could have." His expression is masklike, but it's not his usual polite one. This one says he's very, very angry but not letting himself show it. He might not even be letting himself feel it.

"I shouldn't have gotten in his face," I say. "I should have kept my head, been diplomatic. I lost control."

A muscle in Paul's jaw twitches, but his hands remain gentle. "That's not what I meant. You were amazing. Glorious. You gave Fuchs everything he deserved. I mean…" He takes a long breath through his nose. "This. You shouldn't have to go through this after. I don't like it."

My eyes widen. He doesn't sound embarrassed. He sounds… hurt. Furious. Like my pain is his. "I made a scene," I remind him quietly. "I still am."

I'm unsuitable is what I'm telling him and myself. Amelia would never do something like this.

"Good." The harsh satisfaction in his tone makes my skin tingle. "He deserves a much more public humiliation than that." He lifts his thumb to my chin, tilting my face toward his. "And you take all the time you need here. Do you want me to clear everyone out?"

It takes me a moment to hear what he's said because his eyes are so mesmerizing. They're not quite black actually, but a gray so deep it looks endless. Limitless. The night sky if you could mix the stars into it.

What was he saying again? Yes, kicking everyone out.

I glance around at the nearly full café. All the customers are bent over a screen, pecking away at their keyboards or scrolling through something. "Even if you could, I don't think these people want their work interrupted." When his mouth twists guiltily, I nod. "Right. You own this building, don't you?"

"The family does. But yes."

He's let go of my chin, and his grip on my hand is loose. I feel the chills nipping at my spine again. And they're not coming just from my encounter with Fuchs—there's his family and what I'm supposed to be pretending and the fact that all this will end very soon.

I'm going to miss this place, my life here… and him. I'm definitely going to miss him, more than I should.

"I'm okay." I pull my hand back, pick up my tea. I duck my head to take a sip and almost moan when I do. This is seriously the best tea I've ever tasted.

Paul continues to watch me. I smile back. "I promise I'll be perfectly fine by tonight."

"We're not going." His tone is curt, but I don't think he's mad at me.

"But your mother—"

"No. We're doing whatever you want tonight." He breathes out, his expression softening. "Think about the thing you'll miss most here, and that's what we'll do. Or the place you most wanted to visit but couldn't. No matter where it is." He shrugs. "We can take the jet."

He's blowing off his family for me. Yes, it's just for one night, and the event is dinner at a cousins' house, nothing too major, but it feels very significant. I'm hired to fake it, whenever and wherever he wants. What I want wasn't part of the bargain.

"Thank you," I say gruffly into my tea. I should tell him no, it's fine, but there *is* something I've been wanting to see. Something I won't be able to see back home, at least not exactly like this.

Paul might even like it himself. Or he might be horrified by it.

Actually, probably not. Anyone who willingly hangs out with Finn will probably appreciate this.

"Well?" he prompts. "Think big."

I am, but not in the way he's suggesting. "Well, there's this event…"

Three hours later, we're sitting in a high school gym, the metal bleachers cold and hard. The seats are only half-filled, so every noise bounces off them, the walls, and the high ceiling until my ears are ringing.

The skeptical look on Paul's face has been there since I told him where I wanted to go. "I don't think I've ever been inside an American high school." The curl of his lip says he isn't planning on visiting another one anytime soon.

"You didn't go to high school here?" I thought we went over that when we were making up our grand love story, but I can't seem to remember it.

"No." He's staring up at a banner that declares the Lady Timberwolves were some kind of basketball champion from 2010–2011. "I was at the American School until high school, then came over here when I got into Stanford. My mother thought Harvard was more appropriate, but I liked Stanford better."

Wow. He makes it sound like picking between two of the most prestigious schools in the world is like trying to decide where to go for lunch. I suppose he always knew he'd have his choice of universities, that the entire world would be at his feet, the way it always has been.

"She can't have been that upset," I say. "Stanford isn't exactly a step down."

A smile crosses his face. "Actually, she was furious. Didn't speak to me for the entire first quarter. I had to pay my tuition from some money an uncle left me."

"Your mother did that?" I swivel on the bench to face him fully. "Wait, *you* actually rebelled? Went against your mother like that?"

"I was younger then." He looks like he's remembering his younger self fondly and wistfully. "And it was what I really wanted."

"What made her start talking to you again?"

A rumble comes from the crowd near one of the exits, a flurry of excitement. The entertainment must be starting soon. I ignore it, focusing on Paul and his answer.

"My aunt here—her sister—told her how well I was doing in school, how good Stanford was for me. My mother might seem like a tyrant, but she truly does wants what's best for us. So she relented."

His brow, which is normally so smooth, is wrinkled. This story, while it worked out all right, is still upsetting to him. If his aunt had never said anything, would his mother have ever made amends? Perhaps he wonders the same thing.

"I'd met Mark," he goes on. "No one knew who I was, at least beyond a dozen or so people, and that was freeing. No one to report back to my mother, no one watching to ensure I was always and forever acting as I should be. They say you change in college—at least they do here—and it was true."

He makes it sound like he escaped a prison when he came to college. Which I understand—this was an escape for me too.

And now we both have to go back.

"You don't have to leave it behind forever," I say. "You'll be able to come back and visit."

I probably won't though. I breathe through the pain because I want to enjoy this night. And savor Paul's reaction to it.

"It's not—"

He's cut off by a blast of music from the bank of speakers next to the ring set up in the center of the gym. Paul winces while I grin.

"That's Kane Griffen's music," I shout into his ear.

"They all have their own music?" he shouts back. "And what kind of name is Kane Griffen?"

"A wrestling name."

The gym doors slam open as a fog machine does its best to shroud the entrance in mystery. The figure in the smoke and darkness is massive, muscles bulging even in the shadows.

"I've come for my revenge," a deep voice booms through the gym. "Fenix, your time's up. Tonight."

I hold my breath even though I know what's going to happen next.

A cackle comes through the speakers, low and creepy. "Never. You'll never take me down."

Kane comes running up the aisle, searching for the source of the voice. "Where are you? Face me like a man!"

The cackle comes again, Fenix mocking Kane's challenge. Fenix badly injured Kane's best friend with dirty tricks in a match a few months ago, and Kane's been trying to make him pay ever since. Tonight the big showdown is finally supposed to happen.

Kane keeps looking for Fenix, and Fenix keeps mocking him from somewhere in the wings. I know the match won't happen until the very end of the night, but I still hold my breath as I watch the scene play out. I can't help but be caught up in the drama as the music swells, Kane dissolving into frustrated rage when his revenge remains out of reach. With one last shout, his entire body flexing, he yells for Fenix, then disappears through the gym doors.

The music dims for a minute as the stagehands rush around, setting up for the coming match.

"This is what you're going to miss from America?" Paul is even more skeptical now. "Wrestling's fake."

I roll my eyes. "Really? I never noticed." I hold up a hand when he tries to talk again. "Don't think about how it's fake. K-dramas are fake, but you like those, right?"

"*Like* is a strong word."

Oh, right. God forbid he admit he likes trashy TV. "Wuxia is also fake."

He splutters in indignation, the first time I've ever seen him actually flustered. And speechless. "It's… That's… That's not the point, to be real!"

I seem to have touched a nerve. I hide my smile. "Wuxia movies aren't real. But you still like them."

"Of course I do." His indignation hasn't settled at all.

"Well, this is like a K-drama crossed with wuxia and then drenched in American sauce." It's ridiculous and loud and very clearly acting, but I love it all the same. These wrestlers can jump and flip and fall, and none of that is faked.

"American sauce?" He cocks an eyebrow.

"Yes. Ranch dressing, in fact."

He laughs as he turns back to the ring. The first match is finally beginning, with two guys I don't recognize squaring off against each other. They're not quite as polished as Kane or Fenix, their moves more hesitant, less fluid. And way less acrobatic. But they have potential, and one is super committed to his character, which makes me grin. I love it when the performers are so clearly enjoying themselves.

"Are these guys professionals?" Paul asks as they leave to cheers and waves. "This is definitely not *WrestleMania* or anything."

I shake my head. "No, this is a backyard wrestling league. Guys who just love it and want to do it however they can, wrestlers looking to break into the big time. It's not as glitzy or well produced, but I think it's more fun."

He makes a noise that's supposed to be skeptical, dismissive, but I can hear the curiosity too. This is more fun than he was expecting.

We watch the next two matches without talking much, sharing a package of Red Vines as we cheer on our chosen champions. Paul is slowly getting into it, yelling loud enough to surprise me at a particularly impressive move.

Rather than tease him about it, I yell my approval too, then pass him the Red Vines.

By the time we reach the climax of the fourth match, Paul's on his feet with the rest of us, shaking his fist when it looks like the heel might escape his well-deserved fate. But finally, finally, good prevails with an awesome suplex. The ref counts off, and when he hits three, the entire crowd releases a sigh.

Then the place erupts in cheers.

"Holy shit," Paul says to me as he claps. "Did you see that? It was amazing."

"I did." I clap myself as I watch him. He's grinning like I've never seen before, simply pure, aggressive joy. He still looks noble, but more like a prince at play. Not one burdened with running a kingdom. Or a family. "I figured you'd like it."

His hands slow, then stop, his expression going serious. "I do. Thank you so much for bringing me."

His gratitude is so heartfelt it makes me ache. I swallow past the tightness in my throat. "It was nothing. And now you can come back anytime you're here in the Bay Area."

"There's probably wrestling in China now too."

I shrug, trying to pretend it's no big deal. "There is. It won't be quite the same as here though."

"No," he says thoughtfully. "It wouldn't be."

A hint of music comes through the speakers, swelling and rising. As it does, the crowd goes completely silent. The music marches on, building into Kane's theme.

When Kane comes out, the crowd loses its mind. It's a smaller group, but we're all so invested in this show it feels like there are ten times as many of us.

This is what we've all been waiting for. And when Fenix appears, we know it's on.

The match is everything I hoped it would be, full of highs and lows and amazing, jaw-dropping moves. This might not be professional wrestling, but I'm supremely entertained. And moved too—when Kane finishes off Fenix, I feel his triumph sizzling through my own veins.

Paul does too. Somewhere in the match he's taken my hand, squeezing it tight each time it looks like Fenix might slip free again. But now he's squeezing it tight with anticipation as we both watch Fenix on the floor of the ring, waiting to see if he'll get up this time.

The ref counts to three. Fenix doesn't move.

Kane throws his massive arms up in victory, smiling through his exhaustion. He's done it. His quest is over.

I toss my arms around Paul, too happy to care if I'm being a dork. He holds me close, his body hard and hot against mine. A shiver runs through me, heated and ticklish.

When his mouth finds mine, I'm more than ready. He kisses me deeply, unthinkingly, nothing but emotion between us. This is our triumph right here, our bodies meeting, surrendering to this need.

As the crowd continues to cheer and stomp, Paul kisses me as if we're the only two people here, his tongue tangling with mine, his chest vibrating as he groans into my mouth.

He lifts his head too soon, leaving me panting and needy. I don't care if it's a terrible idea or if I'm completely unsuitable or if he'll break my heart when I leave. I have to have more of him.

His mouth flattens, his nose flaring as he looks down at me. "We need to get out of here," he says grimly.

I can't argue.

CHAPTER SIXTEEN

Paul drives us home like he's racing someone. Or something. The car tires actually squeal a few times when he takes the turns.

I'm not afraid—the car is never out of control—but the way his face is set, stern, determined, makes shivers run up and down my entire body. He has a very specific destination in mind, beyond just his house.

When we arrive at his compound, he takes us to another garage on the other side of the house. Of course he has two garages—he's got two stables, so why not?

And I took him to a night of wrestling.

But he liked it.

I don't know what's going through his head right now as he leads me up a set of stairs I haven't seen before. It seems like we're going up to his wing of the house, but I can't be entirely sure. His mood is like a thundercloud around him— dark, electric, and my nerves are sizzling from it.

We see no one else as we climb the stairs, not even a single servant. What excuse did he give his mother for why we didn't come to dinner tonight? Is she waiting somewhere in her wing to confront him about it?

Paul doesn't look like he's thinking of that though. His

hand is wrapped around my wrist, his grip like iron. I'm excited and a bit embarrassed at how hot I find that.

When we arrive at the door to his bedroom, he practically kicks it open, then shoves me inside. I stumble, catching myself only by grabbing at his shoulder.

The contact ignites the air between us. He spears his hand through my hair and kisses me like I'm the only source of air left in the room. Like he'll die if he ever lets me go. I can barely keep up with him, and I kind of don't want to even try. I want to let him consume me.

But I'm not supposed to want that. This was supposed to be a business relationship only.

I force some space between us even though it hurts to do it. My mouth is tingling, my pulse is drumming, and I can't catch my breath.

Paul doesn't immediately let me go. "If you don't want this…" The want in his voice makes it growly, deep.

"We can't." My protest is as weak as my resolve.

"We can do whatever we want." The arrogance in that is insanely hot. "This can be only for us. We don't have to answer to anyone else."

But we do. He has to answer to his family. I have to answer to Immigration. We can't block out the world.

"We don't live just in this room."

"No, but here we can take something for us. Wasn't that the point of coming to this country?" He's relentless. "To carve out a space all our own?" His grip on my waist tightens, reminds me how solid his hold is on me. "We're still here. We still have time. Let's take what we can."

It's not very noble, that sentiment. Those are the thoughts of a conqueror—but sometimes princes start out as conquerors. They take what they want and only after do they settle into ruling it. And sometimes a prince has to fight to keep what's his.

"And after?" I ask. But even as I do, I know it's a silly

question. There is no after for us, which is why we should seize the present, just like he says.

"Don't worry about after." He nips at my mouth, already sensing my surrender. "There's only now."

I sigh and raise my arms to wrap around his neck. I give up and give in because he's right. I do want this, and I'll take it, and I'll let him take me.

God, I want so fucking badly for him to take me. Like when he lost control and bit my lip, only more and worse.

He reaches down and under the backs of my knees, and I'm suddenly in his arms and he's carrying me to the bed. Kind of like in a fairy tale, except fairy tales were never as hot as the expression in his eyes, as wild as the rise and fall of his chest, as urgent as the pace of his steps.

Paul wants me on that bed *now. Immediately.* He can't wait.

When he sets me on the bed, it's not gentle. It's… it's mean almost. But "I'll make you pay in the best, most sexual way." I bounce as I land, and his hand hooks in the waistband of my jeans, reminding me that he's not letting go. That I belong to him.

I reach for the waistband, ready to shuck them off.

"No." The ringing command in that makes my nipples hard. "I'm taking them off."

My eyes roll back because he's so mean and sharp and just vicious. Or at least he sounds that way. The prince is gone and the conqueror has taken over.

I never knew Paul has this in him. I never knew I could bring it out in him.

With a rough jerk, he unbuttons my jeans, then tears them off me. His usual grace is entirely gone. There's only needy desperation in his movements now.

"I've wanted you for so long." He grinds that out as he stares at my bare legs, starting at my ankles, then slowly, reverently following the lines of them to where I'm swollen and wet for him. "So long. You haunted my dreams."

He makes it sound like it's my fault that happened… and he's going to punish me for it. Punish me with pleasure.

I swallow hard, try to pull air into my lungs. It's too much; he's too intense. I'm going to combust under his gaze. "You did?"

His gaze catches mine, and the jut of his eyebrows says *You know what you did.*

I actually don't—I had no idea I was *haunting his dreams*—but I shiver as I remember our encounters, each and every one. Underneath his cool exterior, while he was discussing horribly boring points of immigration law, *this* was boiling.

"I did." He grabs the hem of my shirt and pulls it over my head. "Don't pretend you don't know how you affect me."

Don't pretend. That's what we've been doing, but not here. Here we're being real and raw, and he's admitting that the effect I have on him is raw and real too.

I stretch, lifting my breasts, shifting my legs, reveling in the surge of power arcing through me. I can bring a prince to his knees. Me.

His breath comes with a sharp inhale, a noise of severe triumph. "So damn beautiful." He runs his hands down my thighs, squeezing with possessiveness. "Beautiful and mine."

He's practically grunting the words, which turns me on even harder. Paul losing control is so unexpected, so glorious, I'm on fire with it.

"Yours," I agree. Because it's so true—I never want another person's hands on me except his.

"Not completely." There's cold stone in his tone as he pulls my panties off. Then comes my bra, and I'm entirely naked.

He doesn't take me in with only his eyes. His hands run over every inch of my skin, as if he means to memorize me by touch. And he's not entirely gentle about it—he takes my nipples between his thumb and forefinger and tweaks, rumbling with satisfaction when I gasp with pleasure.

I'm vibrating from the inside out once he's done, making noises I never have before. Between my legs I'm damp and achy, and I'd touch myself, only I don't think Paul in this mood would like it.

He wants me all to himself. My pleasure is in his hands, not mine.

So I hold back as he finds his way down my body, tracing the lines of my legs from thigh to knee to calf until he settles at my ankles. His hands wrap around my ankles, spread my legs wide, his grip as tight as shackles. My pussy is so exposed, a blush races over my skin.

"You will not move," he says. His brow is one long, deep, stern line. "No matter what I do."

He doesn't ask if I understand or if I agree, because I'm clearly beyond that, my head thrashing on the bedspread even before he's done anything. So cruel, so demanding, so intensely arousing. I'm helpless with need.

When he lowers his head and kisses my pussy, I can't help myself—I buck beneath him. I know I'm not supposed to, but my hips apparently didn't get the message.

He punishes me by lifting his head. The spark in his eyes is wild, unconfined. "You were told."

And then he punishes me by lowering his head and kissing, licking, sucking until I'm out of my mind with pleasure and almost out of my body. I'm one sustained, pitched sensation, and it's too much. Too much.

"I can't. I can't, I can't," I chant, although I have no idea what it is I can't do. Keep feeling like this without shattering?

"You can." Oh, his tone is so stern, so commanding, heat flares in my belly. Paul reaches up, slips one, two fingers inside me and does some kind of twist.

It's too much and more than enough, and I come completely undone. My orgasm rolls through and over me, stealing my breath. And my thoughts.

I'm panting when I come back to the world, sweat

collecting between my breasts and my hair clinging to my cheeks. I must look a mess, but I don't care.

Paul leans over and licks between my breasts, his tongue cool velvet. It's so dirty and unexpected and delicious. "Mine," he says, all his fancy English gone. He repeats it in Mandarin, in case I don't understand. And then in Cantonese. And again in English. "Completely."

He reaches into the drawer of the bedside table and comes back with a condom. His cock is stiff, straining, flushed red with need. Need for me. Once the condom is on, he comes between my thighs, his movements urgent, barely controlled.

His gaze locks with mine. "I'll try to go slow," he says. "At first."

Try. Paul never has to *try* to hold on to his control, but he sounds as if he can barely do it now. I reach for his hips, pull him down and lift myself up, fitting us together in one thick slide.

"I don't want slow," I say. "I want this. You filling me, hard and fast and complete."

His gaze loses focus and he drives into me, his pubic bone catching on my clit with each thrust. We're both heated, glowing with sweat, our skin slapping together with every pump of his hips. God, but there's such power in him; it shocks me all the way down to my toes.

And with the shocks come another rising crest of pleasure. My pussy clenches tight around his cock, and I bite my lip at how full, how deep he is inside me.

"Jesus." He groans, thrusting harder, faster, his hair falling over his brow, his shoulders taut with effort. "Jesus."

I dig my nails into his back, urging him on. He's close and so am I.

At the first pulse of his climax, my toes curl, digging into the bedsheets. At the next pulse, all of me clenches around my oncoming orgasm. And then I'm coming with him, the both of us dissolving into pure bliss.

After, he gathers me close, kissing my hair. Then my eyelids. Then my cheek. His mouth is light, generous, sweet. Cherishing.

The beast is gone, satisfied, and the prince has returned.

I nestle into the crook of his neck, breathing in his scent. He usually smells delicious, something luxurious and clean and smooth, but now he smells… a touch musky. Feral. I love it.

"I should go," I say with a sigh. We might have taken what we wanted in these few stolen hours, but I have to go now. The morning is coming, along with everything and everyone we need to pretend for.

"Not yet." It's a sleepy rumble, but there's a hint of pleading there. Like he knows I'm right but he's not ready to let go.

"Another five minutes," I agree.

We're both asleep before even five seconds are up.

CHAPTER SEVENTEEN

"Paul, where are your clothes?"

I don't spin like a guilty teenager at my mother's voice behind me, the fridge open before me, but I almost do. I'm way too old to jump like I've been caught out. Even though I am trying to be sneaky.

"I *am* wearing clothes," I say idly, pretending to study the contents of the fridge. Track pants and a T-shirt count as clothes, although Mother might not think so. She probably thinks I should never leave my room not wearing a suit.

"I hope you're not going out like that."

I face her, slowly. Like I'm not trying to hide the fact that I came down here to get breakfast for Grace, who's still sleeping in my bed. "No, I'm not. I just wanted something to eat."

"Why are you cooking for yourself?" Mother is already dressed, her hair and face done. She's visibly appalled at my rooting through the fridge. "You pay a chef. Two of them, in fact."

Because I discovered I like doing things for myself. Sometimes. And I was looking forward to bringing Grace breakfast in bed, enjoying the intimate space we carved out together last night.

I sigh and shut the fridge. "I'll call one of them."

Twenty minutes later, my mother and I are eating in the north breakfast nook, not to be confused with the south breakfast nook. The north nook has views of the forest jutting against the end of the estate, while the south nook has views of the valley below.

I managed to snag a passing maid and ordered her to take Grace some breakfast without Mother hearing. I still wish I could have brought it up myself instead of being stuck here with my mother.

We eat in silence for several moments, and it feels… serene. When she's not springing an unexpected fiancée on me, I actually enjoy my mother's company. She's my mother, and I love her in spite of everything.

"Where were you last night?" she asks as she stirs her tea. She picked up the habit of putting milk and sugar in her tea during her years in England, where my father went to the London School of Economics, before I or Lucy appeared. "Auntie May was very put out that you didn't attend."

It's not true—Auntie May is very understanding. And I know for a fact she likes Grace. "Grace wasn't feeling well. I told you."

My mother snorts with delicate grace. "Is she pregnant?"

I choke on my coffee. "No. Jesus, no."

"Good." My mother takes a satisfied sip of her tea. "Because you can't marry that girl."

I go stiff, anger locking my joints. "And why not?"

It takes me half a heartbeat to remember that of course I can't marry Grace and a respectful son would never take that tone with his mother.

My mother's mouth flattens, but she doesn't scold me. "Because she's too nice."

I try to work through that one. "Too… nice?"

"Yes." My mother makes a hand gesture that I think is supposed to make sense. "This family will grind her to dust.

Nice is nice"—she holds up a hand when I start to interrupt —"and I like her very much. And I know that you love her. But your marriage can't be for your benefit alone."

There's a lot to process in there. So much that I struggle to answer. "Of course it's not just for my benefit," I say, but what I can't stop tripping over is *I know that you love her.*

Why would my mother say that? She never comments on my emotional state, not even when I was a kid. And I can't be in love with Grace.

But the part that really gets me is Mother's insistence that I can't marry Grace. It's the only true thing she just said, and it's the point I want to argue hardest. The point that cuts at me the sharpest.

Mother sighs. "If you were staying here, I wouldn't say anything about it. But your wife can't only make you happy. You have to defend this family against outsiders who would harm us and the ones inside the family who'd ruin everything through their own stupidity."

There's a beat where we're both thinking of Archie, although we don't say his name.

"And I'm thinking of her too," Mother says. "Society will be brutal to her. This family will be brutal to her. She's… she's not one of us. And they'll never let her forget it."

"You were one of them, and they fought you for decades when you took over everything."

She blinks, just the once, short and sharp. "That was different. I was a woman. Archie will come around once you're in charge."

"He won't. He's been holding this grudge for decades; he inherited it from his own father. He thinks they were cheated, and he's not letting go."

"All the more reason for you not to marry Grace." Mother gestures with her teacup in triumph. "She doesn't need to spend the rest of her days dealing with him. Or the rest of them."

"But Amelia does?"

Mother's gaze dips briefly. "Amelia knows what she's getting into. And marriage would help her find some… direction."

"Amelia has all the money and time in the world," I say. "If she hasn't found her direction by now, she never will."

Lucy was right: Amelia is a coward. Too much money, too much indulgence. She's never had to take a stand, and she never will.

Grace, on the other hand, has navigated more dilemmas than I ever will. And she's still wrestling with them. The strength in her…

The teacup rattles as Mother sets it on the table. Her expression is drawn, cloudy. Like she doesn't want to say what she's about to. "I realize that perhaps bringing Amelia here was…"

"Too much?" My tone is as dry as her toast.

"You weren't ready for it." She folds her hands, sets them on the gleaming tabletop. "I simply have your best interests at heart. If you'd been born anyone else, you could live the life you wanted here, marry whoever made you happiest. And I wish you could have had that life. But you're my son and your father's son. And that means something. The responsibility for an entire family is a weighty one."

For a moment sadness flashes through her eyes. Regret too. Perhaps she's imagining all the things she might have done after Dad died, things she'd dreamed about. Things that had to be set aside so she could assume responsibility for an entire family.

I wouldn't call my parents' marriage a love match, but they did seem happy in my memories. Perhaps if they'd been given more time together, she could have done those things she's dreaming of with Dad.

I pinch the bridge of my nose. She's right—I was born to a very specific role, one I can't cast aside without hurting the people I love the most. A role that requires a very specific kind of partner.

But when I try to imagine anyone but Grace in that role, it won't work. I'm not only what my mother sees in me or my family, and I'm not only what the Bastards see. I'm all those things together.

And maybe… maybe only Grace can see all of me.

I drop my hand, force my expression to be neutral. "I know that."

"I'm thinking of Grace too," Mother says. The kindness in her voice is a surprise. "It wouldn't be fair to her. She has no idea what it will be like. The attention, the pressure… all of it."

This is my chance to fix all this. To tell Mother that she's right, that I won't be marrying Grace, but Amelia's also not in the running and to give me time to look for a different bride. It's my exact plan, only I can make it happen sooner than expected. If I do it, Grace and I are both off the hook.

And then Grace gives Fuchs the name he wants and her visa problems are gone. It's the happy ending both of us wanted from the very beginning.

Except I can't make myself say it. I can't say *Fine, I won't marry her.*

I can't make this decision for Grace, to continue our charade. It would be a dick move, and she's been pushed around by rich assholes enough—and I'm one of those assholes. But…

But I can't.

Mine. That's what I said to her last night, and it wasn't supposed to leave my bed, but it's here now still. Insistent, real.

"You underestimate Grace," I say. "She can handle anything life gives her. Even our family."

It's true. It's also true that I'm only delaying the inevitable, that we're going our separate ways in only a few weeks. No matter how my subconscious insists that she's mine, it's not happening.

That space we carved out last night is the only place I can think that. But I'm going to be a selfish bastard and keep that space for as long as I can.

And maybe… a plan starts to spin in my mind. Bigger, more ambitious than a simple fake engagement. Something more like a real engagement.

But my mother is right—being my wife won't be easy. My duties will be exhausting, the demands of the business and the family all encompassing. I know I can stand it, but I need to make sure Grace can too.

I'll give it until the gala, keep up the pretense that we're still engaged. I'll see she fits into my life, how much she'll enjoy it. And how well she'll survive more contact with the family. Then I'll propose. For real.

"Paul?" Mother is looking at me as if I've got a fever. Her hand is even hovering in the air between us, as if she's about to check my temperature. "Are you all right?"

I force myself back into the present and out of my planning. "I'm fine. I'm serious about Grace."

Mother's mouth pinches up. "Don't say I didn't warn you. And just remember, divorce is out."

It's not; Cousin Jeffery is on wife number four, and Mother hasn't disinvited him from any of the family gatherings yet. But Jeff's divorces wouldn't be front-page news like mine would.

"No divorces," I say. Which is why I have to make absolutely certain Grace comes into this with her eyes wide open. "Do you think you could be a little more open-minded about her?"

If I am going to marry Grace, she and Mother have to get along. Or at least pretend to.

"I told you I like her." Mother's mouth remains flat.

I'm tempted to tell her to show Grace that, but I know

better. Admitting that even just to me is a big step for my mother.

"I like her too," I say quietly.

It's as much a lie as anything else I've told my mother about Grace—I much, much more than simply *like* her—but my mother hears what I'm not saying, giving me a significant look as she finishes her tea.

CHAPTER EIGHTEEN

I don't think I've ever experienced anything quite like this shopping trip.

Lucy whirled into Paul's bedroom this morning while I was still working on breakfast in bed. My cheeks were flaming at being caught in her brother's bed—with no clothes on either—but Lucy didn't seem a bit surprised.

"We're going shopping!" She tossed back the curtains with the kind of excitement six-year-olds have for Disneyland. "We are going to find you the most gorgeous gown in the world. They will be vomiting with envy when they see you at the gala."

"That doesn't sound good."

She shushed me with a wave of her hand, then whisked me off before I had a chance to see Paul.

Now here we are, in a store so exclusive it doesn't even have a sign. Lucy took us down a back alley in Union Square, lined with dumpsters and the air reeking of something foul, then knocked on a bare door in a specific rhythm.

And then we were whisked into a wonderland.

The store is more like a studio with bare white walls. There are paintings hanging from the walls that look like they're from the Qing dynasty, and I don't think they're reproductions. The images are delicate, elegant, and I'm pretty sure I had to learn some of the poems on them in school.

Lucy and I are sitting on a low couch, each of us holding a flute of champagne. Here I don't have to lift a finger hunting through racks for my size. Everything is brought right to me, and my champagne flute is always full. There's even a dish of caviar on ice next to us, although neither of us has touched it.

I'm desperately afraid I'll spill something on the gorgeous clothes the clerks are bringing out for me and suddenly find myself $50,000 in debt. So I hold myself very still and very far away from the dress spread out before me.

Lucy isn't a bit afraid though. "Come closer. You'll never see it properly from there." She grabs a handful of the fabric and I gasp. "It's so light, but luxurious. And this dress is sexy, but not too sexy. Like you."

"Um..." I shift on the couch. Was that supposed to be a compliment? I think so. Which means I should say thank you. "Thank you." That's too close to a question, so I say again, "Thank you."

Too firm now. The salesclerk gives me an odd look. Clearly she knows I'm very much out of place here.

"You are." Lucy turns to pin me with her stare. "I'm serious. This dress is fresh and beautiful and demure. But also sexy. Just. Like. You."

I lean over, holding my champagne flute as far away from the dress as I can. The fabric is silk, and it moves like water through Lucy's fingers, thick but sensuous. But the pattern is red and pink poppies, and something about it is off-putting. Like it's trying too hard to be... something.

"It's nice," I say.

Lucy doesn't hear the lack of enthusiasm in my voice, probably because she has too much herself. "Try it on. You'll see."

I suppose it couldn't hurt. After all, how often will I get to wear something that costs more than my yearly salary?

The clerk takes me back and has me undressed and in the gown faster than I expect. I shouldn't be surprised though—this is her job and she does it for some of the richest people in the world. Of course she's very accomplished at it.

When I come out, Lucy starts applauding. I smile weakly, then climb up the dais to see myself in the half circle of mirrors there. The silk of the skirt is heavy as I kick my way up the stairs, the poppies flashing red in the corner of my vision.

In the movies, trying on a dress in front of all these mirrors looks glamorous, but I feel more like I'm under a microscope. Pinned like a specimen.

The poppies are overpowering me. All I can see is the dress and the bursts of red and pink on it—my head looks like an afterthought, floating above it all.

Lucy has a hand at her chin, her mouth flat. I can see the professor in her now.

"Hmmm," she says.

"Yes," says the clerk, as if that noise made perfect sense.

They study me silently for a few more moments. "I don't think—"

Lucy shakes her head. "No. No, this isn't it."

It's exactly what I was thinking, but I still feel like I've disappointed them. "Maybe we can come back some other day." We've been at this for two hours, and this is the first dress Lucy has even thought worthy of my trying on. At this rate, we'll be here for the next two weeks, and I'm dying for a nap.

And I miss Paul. I wanted to see him this morning, steal a few more moments together.

Lucy gives me a look, and I know I've really disappointed her now. "Grace. Grace. This is *very* important. We can't leave without a dress. *The* dress. And we won't."

"No," the clerk says, a fervent light in her eyes. "We won't."

"Ooookay." I glance around for an exit. If I make it outside, maybe some passerby will let me use their phone to call January to save me. *If* I make it.

Lucy claps her hands together. "I've been doing this all wrong. I can see why, now that you're wearing that." The silk that she was just caressing so lovingly is dismissed with a flick of her fingers. "Not fresh. Not demure. Dark elegance."

That… doesn't sound anything like me. Like Paul, yes. I'd describe him like that, especially after last night, although not to his sister.

A warm shiver works its way up my back as I remember how he said *mine.*

"I agree completely," the clerk says even though she was saying the opposite a few moments ago.

"Are you thinking…?" Lucy asks.

"I am," the clerk declares.

"The gold velvet," they squeal together.

Lucy turns to me, both excited and relieved. "This is the one. The one we should have put you in immediately."

I have no idea what they're talking about. There's been no velvet dress at all, at least not that I've seen.

"I guess I'll try it on," I say with a definite lack of enthusiasm. Velvet sounds heavy, suffocating. Not me at all.

Lucy's excitement hasn't dimmed a bit though. I thought I enjoyed shopping, but Lucy takes it to an entire other level. One I don't think I can keep up with.

"This will be perfect, I promise," the salesclerk says. "And we'll have just enough time to get it altered for the gala."

I go back and pull off the poppy dress, carefully handing it to a different clerk. I wait and shiver in my bra and panties, trying to imagine what this gold velvet wonder will be like. Will the gates of heaven open when I see it?

What I really want is for Paul's mouth to drop open when

he sees it. I want to look so stunning he can just barely control himself. And after the gala, when we're alone…

My visa expires in forty-some days. I'm going to wring as much pleasure from Paul—and him from me—as I can.

The clerk comes back with the dress draped over her arm, jerking me out of my thoughts. When she shakes it out, revealing the full length of it, all I can do is stare. It's just so…

To call it gold velvet is like calling Paul a thirty-two-year-old man. Yes, both those words would describe him, but neither would capture him. They are literally the blandest things you could say about him.

It's the same for this dress. I reach out to touch the velvet, the nap short but soft. The fabric itself is cool, but as it shimmers, it takes on the color of flames—so many colors at once I can't capture them all. The velvet is possibly the softest thing I've ever felt. I could just wrap myself in it and never leave. Make a little dress cave all for me.

"Yes?" the salesclerk asks. Her smile says she already knows what my answer will be.

I reach for the dress, and she helps me put it on. The magic doesn't disappear once I'm wearing it. It intensifies.

The bodice is fitted, with a high neck that somehow manages to look both enticing and proper all at once. The skirt clings to my hips, then falls in lush folds to the floor. The velvet isn't too heavy—the weight is comforting actually.

I hold out my arms and spin, just for the sheer pleasure of it. As I do, I realize there are panels sewn into the skirt, strips of silk so thin they seem to float under the velvet, catching the light and adding new dimensions to the gown with every motion.

My hair gleams in time with the hidden bits of silk, and I'm almost lit from within by the fire shimmering from the golden velvet, and I feel…

I feel like a princess. Exactly like a princess. Only better, because this is no fantasy.

I spin a few more times, taking in the sheer joy of catching sight of myself in the mirror, the skirt flaring out around me. I wish I were a ballerina so I could just spin forever in this thing.

"Grace?" Lucy calls out from the main salon. "Is it okay?"

I laugh, wild and happy. "Um, it's way better than that."

"Let me see!"

To my eternal delight, Lucy's jaw drops when I come out. I can tell her reaction isn't faked or polite.

"Wow." She actually rises from the couch she's so impressed. "Wow."

I trip up to the dais and swish the skirt for her, showing off the hidden silk. And then I spin some more even though I'm starting to get dizzy. But I'm so in love with this dress I can't seem to stop.

"I think that's the one," the salesclerk says dryly.

Lucy laughs. "She'll be the envy of everyone at the gala. Which is going to make it difficult next year, with everyone trying to outdress her."

I abruptly stop spinning. That's right—this is my one night to shine in this dress. Afterward, I'll have nowhere to wear it. The smart thing would be to sell it, use the money for something better instead of letting it collect dust in my closet.

Just like Cinderella's gown, this thing is going to be unwearable for me after midnight.

"I won't have to worry about that," I say with forced brightness. "I won't be here next year."

Lucy rolls her eyes. "If my brother was smart, he'd propose to you for real. I doubt he will, because he's actually not that smart, but I keep hoping."

My mouth drops open. The clerk discreetly clears her throat and disappears into the back.

"You want *me* to marry *your* brother?" I'm too shocked to keep that quiet or demure.

Lucy narrows her eyes at me. "Don't tell me you don't want to. You're not that good of an actress—you're not faking what you feel for him."

I suppose I should be offended that she doesn't think me that good an actress, but I'm still too shocked at what she said. At how clearly she's seen what I never should have shown. "But I'm not at all suitable."

Lucy huffs out a breath. "Bullshit. Paul needs someone who understands him. Mother's only considering who can best handle the family, but I'm thinking about who can best handle Paul. And not in a controlling kind of way—he deserves to have someone who will always be on his side. Who will understand *all* the parts of him, not just the ones my mother thinks are most important."

I have no idea what to say to that. Of course I would always be on Paul's side, the way he's always on mine. And I suppose I do sort of understand him—he really enjoyed the wrestling.

Afterward, in his bed, we connected in ways I never have before with a man. So… maybe she's right.

"Wow," I say. "That is really profound."

Lucy beams. "I have my moments. I'm usually right about most things. I'm definitely right about this."

She might be, but Paul doesn't see things that way. I'm only a means to an end. Not in a mean, mercenary way—he wouldn't take such good care of me if he were either of those —but our relationship isn't any deeper than that. Even with the sex.

Right?

"Paul doesn't think of me like that." When I say it, I don't sound half as convincing as Lucy did. "You need someone like Amelia, only not in love with someone else."

"I already told you how I feel about Amelia," Lucy says. "You'll do just fine as Paul's wife. My mother comes from a different generation, but you—you'd be the breath of fresh air in his life."

I don't know what to say to that. I love being with Paul, and we had tons of fun at wrestling, which I never expected, and I can definitely see how he needs someone on his side when it comes to family events, and when it's the two of us alone, something magical seems to happen, but...

But there's everything else waiting for us outside just the two of us. "It wouldn't work." I know I'm not going to convince Lucy, but I suppose I'm more convincing myself at this point. "All of this is born out of desperation. Both for him and for me."

The resigned disappointment in Lucy's expression is almost more than I can take, and I'm reminded of how she called Amelia a coward. Perhaps now she thinks I am too.

The salesclerk comes back then, hands full of pins and chalk and a measuring tape. Once she's done pinning and tucking, she takes the dress away. I only just keep myself from protesting, even though I knew the moment was coming. But it's so hard to say goodbye to something that beautiful.

After, Lucy suggests we have lunch at a small, exclusive café nearby. There's an enclosed patio with heaters, and we sit under them and enjoy the most delicious pasta. Lucy talks about everything except Paul, which I'm grateful for.

I'm pondering dessert—tiramisu or gelato—at the end, even though I'm very full.

"They make the gelato here," Lucy says. "It's the best I've had. Outside of Italy, that is."

Because of course she's been to Italy and knows the best gelato places there. If life were different, we might go there together and she could share with me the wonderful things she's found.

There's a shift in the pressure in the air, a subtle press of warmth against my bare skin. And I somehow know without seeing that Paul has walked in.

He has eyes only for me as he makes his way to our table. When he reaches my chair, heat flares in his eyes and I know he wants to kiss me. I want him to kiss me. He dips his head… then pulls back.

"Grace. Lucy," he says too brightly.

Right. He can't kiss me because his sister knows this is all fake. Which means… we're lying to his sister now too. I think.

I touch my forehead, briefly. This is getting too confusing.

"Paul." Lucy looks happy to see him but also puzzled. "What are you doing here?"

"I wanted to see you." Am I imagining it, or did he glance at me when he said *you*? "Both of you."

"We found the perfect dress today," Lucy says as he takes a seat. "You'll love it."

He angles himself so that he's facing me more than his sister. "Did you take any pictures?"

I start to pull out my phone when Lucy gasps. "No. You can't see her in the dress before the gala."

"It's not a wedding," Paul says. There's something underneath his dry tone that makes my heart clench.

Or maybe I'm imagining things now that we've slept together and I'm falling for him. And I've decided to not stop myself from falling for him no matter how terrible that idea is or how badly my heart will break when I leave.

Lucy rolls her eyes. "Right," she mutters. I tense as I wait for her to bring up all her arguments about how Paul and I really should get married, but she thankfully keeps those to herself.

Paul's knee brushes mine under the table. My breath comes in with a tiny squeak. He glances at me with a knowing, secret smile.

He did it on purpose. I'm not at all sure what to make of that, except that it made my heart dance. So I shift, brush my knee against his.

I'm rewarded by another of his looks.

"We've got so much more shopping to do," Lucy says, oblivious to our little game. "I don't know how we'll get everything Grace needs in one day."

"Everything I need?" I cock my head. "What else do I need besides the gown?"

Lucy takes a deep breath, and I can see her preparing a massive list to rattle off. Oh no.

Paul raises a hand, cutting her off before she can even start. "Grace should get only the things she wants." He turns to me. "We'll probably be having family dinners every few days. And there are cocktails with business partners, dinners with their wives, and the press will probably be trying to take your picture everywhere soon."

"The press? But nobody cares about me," I protest. And then it hits me—how often have I seen Paul in the papers and on the gossip sites? The press loves to feature him… and they're going to think I'm marrying him. I swallow hard. "You didn't tell anyone, did you?"

"He doesn't have to." Lucy folds her hands and leans over toward me. "Our family will tell everyone, and the press will pick it up very soon."

I look down at what I'm wearing, suddenly appalled by the white blouse and skinny teal jeans I picked out this morning. "I can't be photographed in this!"

"My point exactly." Lucy gives me an assessing look. "Although, it's actually fine. You'll need some sunglasses. Very large ones. Always have them on whenever you leave the house."

Paul shakes his head at her. "You don't have to do every-thing this tyrant commands," he says to me. "Pick whatever you like best." And then, in front of his sister and everyone, he takes my hand, squeezes it.

I can't tell if he's pretending or not. The heat in his eyes, the… the affection…

"Whatever you choose will be perfect," he says.

And I believe it.

Paul is a very different person when he's with his friends.

Which of course he is; we all are. But seeing him with the Bastards, being part of the group as someone they trust, is a revelation. He laughs louder, longer, makes cruder jokes, sits more loosely with them.

He touches me more when he's with them.

We're at Logan and Callie's house, having just finished an intimate dinner with them, Mark and January, and Finn and Doc. It's a couples-only night, and Paul and I are one of the couples. Everyone's in the living room, chatting and lounging as we digest our dinner, and Paul's arm is draped over my shoulders as we sit together.

Not the back of the couch, close to my shoulders, but on my shoulders.

If anyone thinks it's strange that we're acting like we're together even when they know we're supposed to be faking, no one lets on. No, we're simply accepted as another couple in the group, no questions asked.

Maybe the other guys have already talked to Paul about it. I have no idea what he might have told them. That we're sleeping together while we can? That it's fake outside his bedroom, but very real inside?

Judging by the gleam in January's eye, she very much wants to ask me about it, but she's holding back. I don't know what I'd tell her though. I'm falling for him, and I can almost see a future for us... except for the fact that his mother still hasn't warmed up to me, the rest of his family hasn't either beyond Lucy, and I've got huge immigration issues too.

Oh, and I haven't breathed a word of any of this to my parents. When I talked to them yesterday, they laughingly told me they saw a picture of Paul the other day with a girl who looked very much like me except she was dressed like a queen and Paul looked very much in love. Had he fallen for my twin?

They laughed about it because of course their daughter would have told them if she was dating *the* Paul Tsai. She'd never keep something like that from them.

"Do you know who she is?" Mom asked. I lied and said I had no idea, which they accepted, because of course *the* Paul Tsai wouldn't tell me about his latest girlfriend.

I changed the subject as quick as I could. I already disappointed them with no news about my visa status, so they didn't linger on my prettier, luckier twin. The one dating *the* Paul Tsai.

The Paul Tsai shifts next to me, pulling me closer to him. We're connected from shoulders to thighs, as close as lovers.

"Have you told Grace about the time you tried to tightrope walk over the Terman Fountain when we were at Stanford?" There's a teasing twist to Mark's smile.

Paul shakes his head. "She doesn't want to hear that story."

I set my hand on his knee. "Actually, I do. You *tried?*" I sense there's a very good story behind *tried*, one involving a dripping wet Paul.

"Thanks, man," Paul says to Mark.

Mark shrugs. "That's what I'm here for: to bring up embarrassing stories from your past."

I've already been hearing stories of Paul's past from his relatives. But those stories are about when he was young—a little boy, a teenager, barely a young man—and they all revolve around what a good son Paul was. Doing well in school, respecting his elders, always thinking of others before himself. They're lovely stories since Paul can be a lovely person, but he can also be wild.

I saw some of that at the wrestling night. I want to see some more.

"There are these fountains at Stanford," Paul says. "Terman is a long, rectangular one, almost like a pool."

"Whoa, whoa," Mark said, interrupting. "You're not starting with the best part."

Paul groans. "That's not the best part at all."

"It is," Mark insists. He turns to me. "Our sophomore year, Paul got really into slacklining."

I pull a face without thinking. "*Slacklining?*"

When Paul puts a hand over his face, my cheeks go hot. I didn't mean it to sound so… horrified.

"I mean, I've seen people do it," I say quickly. Mostly overgrown-boy-type programmers who take off their shoes and set up slacklines everywhere they can. They also like to get into a circle and kick around a tiny ball. I don't quite understand it. "It looks… fun."

"It looks dorky," Mark says, correcting me. "And Paul looked dorky. Trust me."

I can't really imagine it, Paul with his shoes off and his arms stretched out, weaving as he tries to stay on the slackline. He would never allow himself to look so silly. But he must have, once upon a time.

"I'm sure he didn't look *dorky*," I say loyally.

Paul squeezes me. "I did. And he's right, I was obsessed. I was walking on that stupid thing every chance I got, trying to go farther and farther. To become the world's best slackliner."

That sounds more like him, that pursuit of perfection.

"So one day," Mark says, "I dared him to walk on the rope across the fountain."

"I thought I was hot shit, so I said yes," Paul says dryly.

"What happened?" I can guess, but I want to hear the gory details.

"I actually did really well. At first."

Mark starts to laugh, trying to hold it in. "Yeah. At first. But then Lucy came by."

I frown. "Lucy was at Stanford?"

"Yeah, she was a freshman. My mother would only allow her to go to Stanford since I was there and could keep an eye on her."

That really sounds familiar.

"Paul's halfway across the fountain when Lucy sees him," Mark says. "And she starts to sneak up on him."

"It wasn't hard," Paul says defensively. "I was focused on other shit."

"Anyway, she reaches one end of the line without him seeing," Mark says. "And she just grabs the line and shakes as hard as she can."

I put my hand over my mouth. It's both hilarious and horrifying all at once. "Were you hurt?"

Paul laughs. "No. But I landed right on my ass in the middle of that fountain."

"He looked like a rag doll when he went down, just limbs going everywhere." Mark rubs at the smile on his face. "And I remember I offered to toss her in for you."

"And I said no. I couldn't do that to my sister even if she was a massive brat."

The affection in Paul's voice is thick. It makes my throat tight. He loves his sister so much, even when she's making him fall into the middle of a fountain. And he won't even toss her in for some revenge.

"Speaking of Lucy"—Mark's voice is casual, markedly so—"how's the uh, family stuff going?" He gestures to the nonexistent space between us.

I suppress the urge to jump away from Paul, because that would look even worse than snuggling close to him.

"It's fine," we both say together. And it really is. So far his family seems to be buying it. They might not have entirely warmed up to me—his mother will speak to me but doesn't seek me out—but no one's denounced me as an imposter or accused us of faking.

Turns out we're pretty good at pretending to be together.

Finn raises his eyebrows. "You guys have really got the acting part of this fake engagement down."

Paul goes very still. "Grace and I get along really well. We're not acting."

"His family is used to me by now," I say quickly, determined to change the subject. "They're all too polite to be rude."

"They like you," he says quietly. "Trust me."

Maybe. But it doesn't matter, because we're not actually getting married. Even if I can see myself with him forever and can handle dealing with his family. I've managed it so far.

"Who wouldn't like Grace?" January says.

"Arne Fuchs," I say.

That gets a grim laugh from everyone.

"Have you gotten anywhere with the leaker situation?" Doc asks. "I wish I could be more help."

I shake my head. "I've narrowed it down to a few possible names, but there's no definitive clues there."

Everyone goes quiet, clearly upset for me.

Paul sets his hand over mine. "We'll keep working at it.

You've got two weeks left. That's plenty of time to find something."

His faith makes hope surge in me. Throughout all this, Paul has never given up, never once said surrender. He's fought beside me, never flagging.

"I haven't quit yet," I say to him. *I won't give up if you won't.*

"I know you won't," he says. The room seems to shrink to just the two of us.

I'm so tempted to kiss him, but I hold back. We'll have plenty of time for that tonight, when it's only the two of us in his bedroom. Instead, I snuggle into his arm and try to forget that I'm supposed to be pretending.

CHAPTER TWENTY

"I hate my family."

I fall back onto the bed, landing right next to Grace. She reaches over and pinches me.

"You do not. Besides, what could they have done now? We finally have a night just to ourselves."

It's the evening before the gala and Grace is right—there's no dinner with the family, no drinks with a business associate, no charity auction to attend. Just the two of us, nestled in my suite of rooms.

The past three weeks have been... beyond belief. Grace hasn't always fit easily into my life—certain members of the family, such as Archie, remain suspicious of her, though Mother hasn't said anything more about my marrying her. But Grace tries. Each and every time, she tries until eventually she fits.

It helps that Lucy is her greatest champion. Most everyone in the family loves Lucy—it's good to be the baby—so if she loves Grace, then they should too.

Actually, Lucy isn't quite Grace's greatest champion: I am. Because Grace... Grace gets me. We walk together into a family gathering and instantly she's running interference, making sure that I hear from the loved ones I need to and that I'm not bothered by the ones I don't. Along with caring for those people I don't always have the time to properly attend to, like Auntie May.

It's exhausting, for her and me, but she makes it better. We've learned to lean on each other.

And when we walk out, she's ready with something just for us. Like a wrestling video or tickets to a show she heard about or even simply watching TV. Apparently the guys behind *The Simpsons* made a show about the future and it's hilarious. I never would have simply sat down and watched some cartoon series on my own. But with her, I love it.

"They won't stop texting me about tomorrow night," I say. "I've already gotten five requests for pictures of your gown."

She props her chin on her hands. "Did you tell them you haven't even seen it yet?"

It's sitting in a garment bag inside my walk-in closet. I've never been so tempted to open something early, not even my Christmas presents when I was a kid.

"No, I told them to ask Lucy for pictures." I snort as I imagine her reaction to those requests.

Grace laughs, but she also says, "You should be nicer to your sister. Especially since she got your mom to stay with her."

True, I do owe my sister big-time for that. Lucy, who sees way more than she should, must have guessed at my plan to woo Grace. Otherwise, she'd have never asked Mother to stay at her place.

"You always stay with Paul," she said to Mother the day after she went dress shopping with Grace. "It's not fair. My house is nice too."

I bit my lip to keep from laughing, because Lucy has never wanted Mother to stay with her before. And also not to piss Lucy off since she was doing me a solid.

"Well, all right," Mother had said, looking only slightly

confused. And as Lucy ushered Mother into her car, ready to take her to her house, my sister leaned over to me and whispered, "Don't blow this."

I don't think I have. Grace is glowing, her cheeks pink with laughter and happiness. And she's been looking like that more often than not.

Maybe I've convinced her that she has a place in my life. I'm certainly convinced.

"Lucy is a monster," I say. "I'm never budging on that."

Grace rolls over, snagging her phone from the bedside table. "I'm ordering pizza."

I point to the house phone. "Use that. The chefs will cook up whatever you want."

"No." She shakes her finger at me as she puts her phone to her ear. "We're getting delivery."

I can't help the face I make. "Really? Why would you do that?"

"Because it's good." She moves the phone from her mouth and frowns at me. "Have you ever had delivery pizza?"

I actually haven't. Somehow, all throughout college and after, when we were building Bastard Capital in a garage, I avoided delivery pizza. It just looked so… unappealing.

"Oh my God, you haven't," she says. "We're definitely getting it."

An hour later, I'm working on a slice of pepperoni—my third—and we're several episodes into a *Futurama* binge watch. Grace is curled up next to me, and we're both propped up in my bed. It's cozy, unfussy, and quite possibly the simplest way we could spend our evening.

My mother would be horrified if she knew I was eating in bed. And delivery pizza no less. Even Lucy would be skeptical.

I love it. I've never done this with a woman, watched silly TV and eaten greasy food, and I never would have if it weren't for Grace.

If I marry the kind of woman my mother thinks I should, I never will again.

The episode ends, and I set my crust aside, wiping my hands on a napkin. If I were being polite, I'd eat the entire thing, but I don't have to be polite and I don't like the crust. So I have the freedom to not eat it.

Grace sits up, her expression going cloudy. Like a weight is settling on her.

"What's up?" I ask. If she's worried about the gala tomorrow, she shouldn't be. She'll be perfect and wonderful, and everyone will love her.

I've decided to bring up a real engagement with her right after we announce our fake one. She has to know how well she fits into my life by now. We'll figure out the immigration thing, go see my family in Taipei, see her family in Beijing, figure out our life together. If she can't come back… Well, she'll like Taipei once she sees it. And we can spend part of the time in Beijing too.

She shifts, a faraway look in her eyes. "I've been thinking about what Fuchs said. About the mole."

I tense up because I've been trying not to think about that. I know she's been going through the files, still searching for clues, but she hasn't said anything more about it. I figured she hadn't come up with a name, and I didn't want to press her on it. I want her as my wife with or without a green card.

Although I still think she should give Fuchs a name. She doesn't owe anyone at that company anything, even if they did help Doc and Finn.

"What about it?" I keep that neutral.

She presses her lips tight together. "I don't think I can give him what he wants."

"Because you can't figure out who sent it?"

She picks at the bedspread. "Partly. I've looked and looked and looked again, but I can't pin down exactly who it is." Her gaze meets mine, open, vulnerable. "But even if I could, I couldn't give Fuchs the name. It's just… I can't."

Her eyes begin to fill with tears, so I pull her into my arms, settling my chin on her head. She's so soft, smells so delicate. I want to never let her go.

"It's all right." Somehow I knew she wouldn't. It just isn't in Grace to do that. Not even to save herself.

"I know you wanted me to and it would be easier if I did, but I just can't."

"It wouldn't be easier if it would tear you up inside." I kiss her hair. "And don't do it because I want it."

"I don't want to disappoint you."

My heart takes on a weight, stretching and straining. "Grace." I tip her chin up, look into her dark eyes. "You've never disappointed me. And you never could."

"Paul." She says my name the same way I said *mine* to her —filled with possession and need. So I kiss her, deep and hungry.

Her response is a wonder, putting her hand to my cheek and drawing me closer. But it's not enough; she's in the wrong place.

I flip her onto her back, rear up over her. The flare of heat in her eyes makes my cock stiffen. I can be demanding, greedy here, not at all noble or kind, and she *loves* it. I can be anything and everything with her.

I rake my teeth down her neck, across her collarbone, because I want to devour her. I want to set her aflame, watch the pleasure burn to ash, then do it all over again. She moans, opening her thighs wider, cradling more of me.

I slip a hand under her shirt, find her sweet breasts, tease a pert nipple. She writhes, lifting her hips. I roll her nipple between my fingers, and she goes even wilder.

Then she grabs my shirt by the collar and rips it. Just *tears* it, like she's so goddamn mad it's covering me. She's not quite strong enough to tear it completely in two, but she's gotten her point across. I'm amazed and amused all at once.

In a flurry of hands and arms and legs, we strip as quickly as we can. I should be making this slow, reverent, properly romantic for my future bride, but I'm almost out of my mind with need, and Grace is just as worked up.

"Hurry," she urges once she's entirely naked—God, but she's beautiful—and I'm still working on my shorts.

"I'm not going anywhere." But I speed up anyway, my cock bobbing painfully once it's free. Only she can get me as hard as this, hot as molten lava and ready to go off like a firecracker. We've been fucking every night for weeks, and it gets more urgent each time.

She grabs a condom and swats my hand away when I reach for it. I smile at the show of her claws. And then I groan, because she's grabbed my cock, stroking from root to tip, not at all shy about it.

I thrust into her hand because if I don't, my brain will explode. Her fingers are delicate, cool, but the motion of her hand is anything but.

"I love you like this," she says.

My heart and brain stutter in time because she's said that word. *Love.* "What?" My tongue is thick, stumbling, same as my thoughts. Jesus, her hand…

"You're so lost to this," she says. "Just my hand, touching you, but it utterly transforms you." The wonder in her voice, her expression, is a stab to my heart. "And only I get to see it."

I kiss her then because what's she said is so goddamn true that kissing her is the only response. I should be proposing now, sealing this moment, but I can't. My desire has completely taken over, and I can't even find the words to tell her everything I want to.

Time. I still have time. For this and proposing and everything else I want to do with her.

So I let her roll on the condom and join myself to her. Join us together.

Her entire body fits me, her pussy tight, hot, her legs coming around my hips, her breasts against my chest, her arms looped around my neck. She lifts up to meet my thrusts, taking me deeper and deeper.

We're in the most perfect harmony, and I can't tell who comes first, her or me. Or if our orgasms are too deeply intertwined to ever know.

Tomorrow, after the gala, I'm going to make sure that the rest of lives are just as intertwined.

CHAPTER TWENTY-ONE

I was so nervous the morning of my university exams that I threw up. Three times.

But I've never been so nervous as I am now. I'm backstage with Lucy at the gala, and Paul's about to announce to the cream of San Francisco society and his extended family that we're getting married.

I meant it when I said I didn't want to disappoint him. Because... because I love him.

It came to me sometime today, even though I've been feeling this way about him probably since I first met him. I couldn't see him at all today—Lucy whisked me off early to start getting ready, and apparently you really *can* spend eight hours primping for a party—and I missed him. Desperately.

And I almost emailed Fuchs a couple of times and told him who I thought his mole was. I knew doing that would make me hate myself, but I love Paul so much I would do almost anything to stay with him.

Except getting my visa approved doesn't mean a happy ending for us. Paul's still leaving. He's still the heir to a massive fortune and weighty responsibilities. And while I think I've done a good job being his partner, none of it's been real. The sex was, but that isn't enough.

But maybe there was more that *was* real. Yes, yes, there was. I know there was.

"Hey." Lucy taps my arm, interrupts my whirling thoughts. "There's nothing to worry about. Smile."

I can't though. This is the moment Paul and I have been working toward for weeks now. My nerves are too twisted to unknot. "I'll smile when I get out there."

Lucy rubs my arm, just like a real sister would. She says nothing else, which I'm strangely grateful for. Having her here, giving me silent support, means more to me than I thought possible.

The emcee is speaking now, calling for everyone's attention. He asks if everyone's having a good time—they politely applaud *yes*—and if they've been enjoying the entertainment. When he introduces Paul—"the new head of Tsai Holdings and your host tonight"—the polite claps grow louder, more sincere.

"While we'll all miss Lillian"—the emcee pauses for the applause—"we all know Paul will continue her legacy of support for the foundation. And this wonderful event."

It will be all over the financial papers tomorrow, the story that Lillian is stepping down and Paul is taking her place. It will be accompanied by pictures of this party, of the Tsai family united, dressed in their best, and giving back to the most needy. His mom really is a PR genius.

And I have to play my part by standing beside Paul and looking like the supportive, adoring fiancée.

I don't think about how it has to end soon, about how my visa expires in mere days. I can't, not if I'm going to pretend my heart out here.

Paul steps into the spotlight, thanking the emcee for his introduction. He's in a tux, and the stark lines and lack of color only emphasize how handsome he is, a frame for his perfect beauty. His picture from tonight is going to cause many a girl to swoon when she sees it.

He waves the crowd, acknowledging their applause without seeming to encourage it. "I want to thank you all for being here," Paul starts out. Of course he began with a thank-you; he always has perfect manners. "Thanks to the funds you've raised tonight, many lives will be saved."

He turns, his gaze searching for something in the wings.

"That's your cue," Lucy whispers, pushing me forward.

When Paul sees me, something comes over him. His polite mask slips, and there's... pure amazement. Open wonder.

"Grace," he says, but not into the mic. Just for me. And then he holds out his hand to me.

Lucy doesn't need to push me—I'm already going toward him, my own hands reaching out. He pulls me close when I arrive, closer than he needs to.

I can hear gasps from the audience, even a few *awws* when Paul dips his head as if he's going to kiss me.

He doesn't though; he simply watches me. His gaze is intense, potent. Not his look of fake adoration, but something more real.

My heart slows way down, almost stopping. He looks like he's really in love with me. Like I'm in love with him.

"When all this is done," he says only to me, "we need to talk. About the future."

Everything that was swirling in me before—my feelings, my doubts, my indecision—stills.

"Okay" is all I can manage to say. I can't think of anything better while I'm trying to interpret his expression and hold on to my smile.

He turns me toward the crowd, loosening his hold so that they can see me better. I put on the smile I've been practicing for days—polite, demure, appreciative, no teeth. And remember to tuck my chin, angle myself toward Paul. All the better to photograph properly.

I think I'm doing it correctly, but I won't know until

tomorrow when I see myself in the papers. My mouth is dry and my heart is thundering, but thank goodness that won't show up in the pictures.

"I'm very pleased to be taking my mother's position at Tsai Holdings," he says. "Her retirement is well deserved, and I hope to lead the company as well as she has in the past. And to honor our commitments to the charities supported by our foundations."

There's some applause there, but I can sense the crowd waiting for what they really want—his introduction of me.

He takes my hand, squeezes it. And takes a moment to simply look at me. I smile too big before I remember not to —*no teeth if you can help it*—but since I was smiling just for him, I couldn't help it.

"I have a more personal announcement too." Paul's not looking at the crowd as he speaks—his gaze is tight on me. My skin warms beneath it. "I'm pleased—honored—to introduce you all to my fiancée, Grace. When she agreed to be my bride, I knew my future would be a happy one."

My cheeks flush because that's more than he needed to say. But he's not done.

"She's truly my better half. And I hope you all"—his gaze sweeps over the crowd—"will join me in welcoming her to our family. I know you will all come to love her as much as I do."

The flush has crawled up my neck and spread over my chest, my ears ringing with his words. *Love.* It feels like no accident he said that. And definitely not fake.

All Paul had to say was that we were engaged, maybe a few words about how happy he was, something light, shallow. That's all anyone would have expected from him.

But to say he loves me…

Everyone is clapping for us, and there are even some cheers as Paul hands the mic back to the emcee. Then he's pulling me offstage and I've never been so happy. Not just to be done with that moment but to be alone with him.

He feels the same; I can tell from his expression. "Finally." He frames my face. "Grace, I—"

"Paul! Grace!" Lucy is coming toward us, along with his mom.

Paul swears under his breath, then drops his hands.

His mother nods to me—I think she's actually approving? —and then tells Paul he needs to speak to the donors. Lucy takes me the opposite direction, telling me how beautiful I looked, how wonderfully we pulled it off, and soon enough Paul and I dissolve into our separate roles at the party.

I can see him sometimes across the room as Lucy introduces me to everyone and I accept their good wishes. He stands out among all the other men even though they're all in tuxes. Or maybe it's just that he draws my eye constantly.

After about two hours of meeting people and saying thank you to their congratulations, I need a break. While Lucy is chatting with one of her school friends, I seize my chance to slip away.

It's not too hard to find the doors leading out to the balcony of the War Memorial Opera House. I've only ever seen the building from the outside before, the elegant columns, high windows, and ornate flourishes. But now I'm one of those lucky people on the balcony, staring down at the people below and the traffic rushing along Van Ness. Across the way, city hall is wreathed in light, the great dome massive and imposing. The balcony is cold after the enclosed heat of the party and the spotlight, but the fresh air feels good. Bracing and head clearing.

When Amelia appears at a side door and walks out onto the balcony, the hair on my arms rises. I've seen her at most of the family dinners over the past few weeks, but she's never said much to me. I got the impression she didn't think I was worthy of her attention and certainly not her jealousy. I don't know what she wants, but I somehow instinctively know it's not good, not if she's seeking me out now.

Which is definitely what she's doing, heading straight for me even if her steps are a little unsteady and her cheeks are deeply flushed. I think maybe she's had one too many glasses of champagne.

She still looks amazing, way more at home in her designer gown than I am in mine. There's a hint of a sneer on her face, but she still looks *so* beautiful.

But even as sophisticated as she is, Paul didn't want to marry her. That thought makes me want to smile even though it's not very kind.

I wrap my arms around myself and debate just running away. It would be terribly rude, but I don't think she means to tell me anything good.

"So, you passed mommy's inspection." Her plummy British accent turns *mommy* into *mummy*. Once upon a time I would've killed for an accent like that.

"I think Paul can make his own decisions without his mother interfering." I cock my head at her. "Don't you?"

Even though she's clearly buzzed, she catches my implication. "I didn't want to marry him anyway."

I laugh because she sounds like a spoiled child. "Right. He's gorgeous and rich and holds himself like a prince, and you didn't want to marry him? Okay."

I've hit a nerve, and she takes two uneven steps backward. "I could have married him. If his mother hadn't tried to force him into it."

"But aren't you in love with someone else?"

She looks away, but not before I see the raw pain flash across her expression. "If Paul had only talked to me before he proposed to you, we could've come to some agreement. We could have been together in public and done whatever we liked in private. It would've been perfect."

I can't hide the revulsion that passes through me. "But if

you love this man, why would you do that?"

She takes a deep, shuddering breath, and I fear for a moment she might start crying.

"Amelia?" I reach out for her arm, but she shoves me away.

"You two are never going to get married," she spits out. "You know that, don't you?"

My heart stops. She's found out our secret. If she tells anyone… But then I realize she's referring to something else.

"You think he's too good for me," I say slowly.

"It's not that he's too good for you, although he is. It's that you have no idea how to operate in this world. This family is going to eat you alive first chance they get. It would really be much better for everyone if you'd just run along now." She makes a shooing motion with her hand, as if I'm an annoying pet or a moth or something.

I know she's saying it just to upset me, but it still hurts. Corvus fired me, the United States government said they don't want me no matter whom I work for, and then to hear Amelia outright say those awful things, on this night that I almost believed I was a princess…

It hurts. It really, really hurts.

But I also know that Paul, underneath his suits and manners, isn't all prince. And that he needs more than a princess by his side.

"You're drunk," I say with all the cold dignity I can muster. "I won't tell Paul about this, but you should leave. I'll even call you a car."

"*Paul.*" She injects a lethal amount of venom into that. "Where is he? If he loved you so much, he wouldn't leave you alone with all these people. People like me. He doesn't really care about you. And as soon as he realizes you can't advance his business interests, not like I can, he'll drop you."

I draw myself up to my full height and stare her straight in the eye. "Lucy was right about you. You need to make up your mind about what you want. You don't want Paul—we both know that—but you're putting on this sad display anyway. You're a coward."

With that I make a sweeping exit, walking down the stairs that lead to the sidewalk and leaving through the emergency gate.

CHAPTER TWENTY-TWO

I'm more than ready to ditch this party.

Before, I never would have dreamed of leaving so early. It would've been rude, and my mother would've been horrified, and of course they would need me to stay until the bitter end. Wasn't I one of the most important people here?

But now I'm just eager to get back to Grace. Stupid of me to plan to ask her to marry me on the one night we can't catch even half a second of privacy.

What can I say though? I can't think straight when it comes to her. She looked so luminous when she came out on stage, I couldn't breathe for a minute. And I almost dropped to one knee and proposed right then and there.

The man next to me has been droning on about his golf game for almost ten minutes now. Or maybe he's talking about a golf course. I haven't been paying attention. Everyone else in the group is nodding along enthusiastically though.

Fuck this. I've done my duty, and now I'm going to take some time—some happiness—for myself. Without a farewell, I leave. Golf Man doesn't even pause.

I see Lucy out among the crowd, laughing at something

one of her friends is saying. I walk up, smile an apology, then pull Lucy away.

She starts to protest, then stops at the look in my eyes. "So you figured it out?"

I don't need to ask what she means. "I figured it out a while ago. I just needed to give Grace some time to get used to the idea. I'm going to propose—for real—tonight."

Lucy is smiling so widely I'm worried her lips are going to crack. "Go then! Tell her now!"

"I've been trying to get a private moment with her for hours. These people won't stop talking to me."

"Oh, poor baby, to be the beloved and desired heir."

I make a face at her since she knows damn good and well she's the spoiled in the family. "Don't worry. I'm leaving now. Can you cover for me?"

"Of course. You're not half so important as you think you are anyway." She shoves me toward the balcony door. "I saw Grace go that way a few minutes ago. Hurry, because I want to celebrate with you guys. For real."

"If she does say yes"—Lucy lifts her eyebrows like that would never happen—"you're not seeing us until tomorrow morning," I say. "At the very earliest."

Lucy's grin is wicked. "Thank God I got Mom out of your house then."

I give her a kiss on the cheek because Lucy really is the best sister I could ever have wanted. "Thanks. I'll let you know how it goes."

And then I sprint for the balcony door before anyone else can grab me. But when I get out there, Grace is nowhere to be seen. There's only Amelia, looking miserable and like she's going to have the mother of all hangovers come morning.

Something in her face puts me on edge. She looks so guilty she could throw up, and not only because she's drunk way too much. I hope my mother hasn't seen.

"What happened here? Where's Grace?"

Amelia spins to face me, clearly shocked by my cold tone. "I was only trying to help her."

The hair on my neck stands up. "What you talking about? What did you tell her?"

Instead of answering, Amelia sits down hard on the floor, her dress billowing around her, dirt streaking the skirt. "He left me." Her voice is barely above a whisper.

"What?" I crouch down beside her. "What's happened?"

Her hands are covering her face, and she speaks around them. "Jin said we couldn't carry on in secret anymore, that he was tired of sneaking around. That if I loved him, I'd have told my parents about him." She takes a sharp inhale. "And since I hadn't, clearly I didn't love him. Not enough. So he said it was over."

Jin has a point as far as I can see. He and Amelia have been carrying on for years; did she really expect him to stay with her like that for the rest of his life? Only meeting in secret and never having a real, full life together?

"What did you tell him?"

"I told him that I could never tell my parents. They'd cut me off!"

I realize suddenly that Lucy's been right about Amelia all along. She's a coward. Not evil or horrible or even a bad person. Just a coward, which is somehow worse.

"I'm very sorry," I say gently. "But where is Grace? I have to find her."

Amelia rubs her eyes like a too-tired child, smearing her mascara. "I was mean to her. So she ran down the steps." And then she breaks into noisy sobs.

I know I should feel bad for Amelia, and I do, but Grace would never do this. No matter how upset or angry or sad she was feeling, she would hold herself together. For me. And I would do the same for her.

And once we were alone, I would hold her and let her cry as much as she wanted.

I take off my jacket and slip it onto Amelia's shoulders. I pull out my cell phone and fire a text off to Lucy, telling her she needs to put Amelia in a private car and send her back to the hotel. And that I have to go find Grace.

As soon as Lucy appears at the door, I sprint down the stairs to the sidewalk. Amelia made it sound like Grace ran off in a tizzy, but that's not like Grace. I'm guessing she took off before she lost it and popped Amelia in the nose. Or did a suplex on her.

Amelia didn't go into detail, but I can guess at some of the things she might have said to Grace, about how she wasn't worthy of marrying into our circle. None of it's true, and I don't think Grace would believe it, but it still must have been infuriating to hear.

She probably just wanted to get away from Amelia and didn't go far.

But when I arrive at the sidewalk, it's eerily empty. There's no fog, the air is as clear as it ever gets, but there's nothing to see. No Grace, not even a hint of her. I walk around the building once, twice, three times, thinking that maybe I just missed her. Maybe she went back inside, maybe she's walking in the opposite direction from me, or maybe we're circling around each other.

But somehow, deep in my gut, I know that she's gone. That I could search the city forever and not find her. There's a hollow spot in my chest that wasn't there before, and it keeps growing.

I head back to the main doors, the hollowness shifting to something like panic. I can't lose my cool, not at this event, not in front of all these people, but if Grace isn't inside—

My phone buzzes from inside my jacket pocket. Grace's name flashes on the screen.

I close my eyes, relief flowing through me. Thank God.

"Where are you?" I'm so keyed up I don't even bother to say hello. "I can't find you."

There's no answer. Instead, it's only dead air. And maybe… scraping.

Or scuffling. Like someone is fighting someone off.

"Grace," I shout into the phone. "Can you hear me?"

I search up and down the street, in case she's nearby. I never once considered a kidnapping attempt. Fuck, I'm so goddamn stupid to not have thought of it, to not have had a dozen security guards following her.

"Stop jerking around." It's a man's voice, coming from far away. "You're not getting out of those cuffs."

My blood turns to ice.

There're more noises, only this time… it sounds like she's in traffic. Or like she's in a car.

"Grace," I call again. I don't think she's actually holding her phone, but hopefully she can at least hear me. "Tell me where you are."

"What the fuck?" It's the man's voice again, closer though. Like he's picked up the phone.

"They're deporting me!" That's Grace, far away, frightened.

Shit. Did ICE grab her? But her visa is still good.

Or did the kidnappers lie about being federal agents?

"Where are you? Can you see anything?" Even just a small clue. I can work with that; I'll find her no matter—

There's a loud noise, like the phone has met the asphalt at high speed, and then the tinkle of broken glass.

And then nothing.

CHAPTER TWENTY-THREE

"Lucy!"

Everyone at the gala turns to stare when I come crashing inside, yelling at the top of my lungs for my sister. Even the music seems to dim.

I'm making a scene, something I never, ever do, and the papers will be filled with this tomorrow instead of our carefully planned announcements, but for once I don't give a shit. Grace is the only thing I care about, and she's out there somewhere, kidnapped by God knows who. Fuck all these people and fuck their respectability.

"Paul." Lucy cuts through the crowd, her face deathly pale in contrast to the deep purple of her gown. "Did you find her?"

I shake my head. Everyone surrounding us is staring openly, and I'm tempted to snarl at them. "She's been taken. I don't know by who. I need to…"

My vast network of friends and associates flashes through my head. I'm the guy who knows a guy, the one everyone comes to when they need something from a certain person. If this happened to anyone else, they'd be coming to me to find out who could help.

So who the fuck do I need to track down? I can't come up

"

with a name. All I can hear is the terror in Grace's voice, then the shatter of the phone.

The immigration lawyers? So far they've all been useless.

All the power brokers I know in Homeland Security? Again, useless.

The politicians I've bought with some well-placed donations, the titans of industry I've laughed with, the tech gurus I've funded—none of them can help me.

I do know some mercenaries though. And they come cheap compared to the lawyers.

Lucy puts her fist to her mouth. "Oh no. He really did it."

"Fuchs?" I take her arm, pull her closer so I can hear her better. The crowd's started murmuring, and I don't have the time to tell them to shut it.

"Fuchs?" She frowns like she doesn't know him. "Oh, Grace's boss. No, *Archie.*"

My rage focuses to a single, sharp point. I've got a target now. And I'm going to make him pay. I was so busy trying to fool my mother—and falling in love with Grace at the same time—I didn't keep my eye on him. I should have known he wouldn't give up without a fight.

"What happened?" I ask with deadly clarity.

"He called ICE on Grace. Said she was here illegally, that her visa had expired." She licks her lips, looking afraid. Maybe of me, maybe for Archie. "One of my friends overheard him telling someone about it. She came to me, wanted to know if it was true." Lucy's voice goes quiet. "If Grace was only marrying you for a green card."

Oh, that's going to be a lovely rumor to have flying. If I weren't so focused on Grace, I'd feel worse about it. This evening is just becoming the perfect shit storm.

"Forget about it," I say. "Grace is gone. I'm pretty sure ICE has her. If it's not them…"

Lucy grabs my arm tightly. "Let's find Archie and confront him."

He's at a table with my mother, talking her ear off while she simply looks bored. I catch a few snatches about a building and real estate prices and acting immediately. The fool is still trying to convince her to fund one of his idiot deals, and he hasn't the eyes to see how badly he's failing.

"Archie."

His head snaps up at my cold tone, his voice dying. For half a moment he looks guilty, guilty as fuck, and I immediately know it's true.

"You son of a bitch," I say, my breath low and taut.

"Paul." Mother's scandalized, but I can't care.

"Tell her what you did," I demand of Archie. "Tell everyone what a sneaking rat you are."

"Everyone is watching," Mother warns.

"Good. A public confession is exactly what I want."

Archie shifts in his chair and swallows hard. "What about your public confession? A fake engagement is certainly not something to be proud of."

My face sags. How the hell did he find out? I glance at Lucy, and she shakes her head. If she didn't tell, and Grace definitely wouldn't have told, how did he know?

"What is he talking about?" my mother asks.

Triumph twitches at the corner of Archie's mouth. "I did some investigating. Grace doesn't have a green card, isn't a citizen—she's here on a visa. One that's about to expire. And no one, absolutely no one, has ever seen the two of you together before you announced this engagement. You two are so in love but apparently never go out in public. Not once. It wasn't hard to figure out—she needed a green card and tricked you into an engagement."

I almost roll my eyes because Archie's so close yet so far. "She's not marrying me for a green card. And she didn't trick me into anything."

My mother is looking between us, and I can see her putting the pieces together, fitting them into the timeline of when she arrived with Amelia in tow. This isn't how I wanted to tell her, but I don't have a choice at this point.

Archie snorts. "Whatever you need to believe."

"Did you call ICE and inform on her?"

My mother gasps but I ignore it, completely focused on forcing an answer from Archie.

He sets his lower lip, which only makes him look petulant. "I did. I told them she'd be here."

Lucy fists her hand into the back of my jacket, anchoring me in place. It's a silent warning to not make an even bigger scene than I already am.

"Why?" The question comes out like the hiss of a dragon's breath.

"To make a point."

"What point?" I'm not sure if Archie hears the horrified anger in my mother's voice, but I certainly do.

"It proves that your son isn't the one to lead the company —if he chooses such an unsuitable wife, what else will he get wrong? No, the board has to understand we can't risk our future with him at the helm." Archie folds his hands as if he's just made the world's greatest argument. "With the scandal surrounding this, you won't be able to cover it up. The board will know, and they won't be pleased."

Mother curls her lip. "The board will do whatever I tell them. Your father would have ruined everything because he was as thickheaded as you are. He might have been rightfully next in line, but it would have been madness to let him take over. And it would be madness to let you do the same."

Archie's jaw twitches. I can't tell if he's furious or about to cry. "But… this girl is completely unsuitable. Even you agree."

Oh, that asshole. I'm halfway out of my seat before Lucy grabs me, sits me back down hard.

Mother folds her own hands in a mockery of Archie's posture. "My son is now the head of Tsai Holdings. The paperwork was completed before I even left Taiwan. That is how much I trust my son's judgment. If he has chosen her, then she is suitable. No matter what anyone else thinks."

My rage at Archie cools, replaced by sour guilt. My mother still thinks my engagement is real. And I never had the chance to make it real because I kept putting off asking Grace, thinking I still had time.

Archie's right—I am an idiot. But not for the reasons he thinks.

"Since he is in charge," my mother says, glancing at me, "he will choose your punishment."

Archie meets my gaze with a defiant glare. I wait for some gesture of apology or even reconsideration, but he's holding strong to his indignation.

Fine. I'll do what I have to then. "You're out of the company. All board meetings, all deals, all future earnings. I can't touch your trust fund"—more's the pity—"but in no way will you benefit from being a member of this family. You are… banished." I shrug since the word is dramatic, but it still fits. "Other family members might invite you to their homes —I can't stop them—but you are not welcome in mine nor at any family gathering I'm attending." I point to the door. "Including this one."

Archie looks between me and Mother, clearly expecting her to step in. Her mouth turns down, and she stares at the exit. He rises, snapping his jacket off the back of his chair. To his credit, he doesn't try to get off any clever parting shots. He just disappears through the door.

After a moment, Lucy asks, "Does anyone have the number for ICE?"

My shoulders slump. "We'll have to go through the lawyers, I think. I've got a bunch of them on retainer luckily."

Grace might already be on her way to Beijing. I could race out to SFO, see if I can stop them at the international terminal, but I'm not certain they would even let me past the security checkpoint. I haven't flown commercial since…

ever. And getting into a fistfight with federal agents would be the height of stupidity even if the testosterone surging through me insists it's an awesome idea.

"Sit down."

Our mother's command is soft, but Lucy and I both instantly sit.

"Explain." She fixes us with the Mother's Death Glare.

Lucy glances at me guiltily. I smile with resignation and relief. It's more than time to come clean.

"Archie's right," I say. "The engagement was fake."

My mother's mouth tenses. "I thought so."

"What?" Lucy and I say together.

"At first," she admits. "The timing was too suspicious. I tell you you must marry, bring a perfect candidate, and you are already engaged? Come now."

I could argue that Amelia wasn't anything like the perfect candidate, but I don't.

"But then at dinner, you seemed... taken with her. I couldn't entirely be sure," Mother says.

"That's why you came to stay at the house," I say. "You wanted to see if we were living together." Wow, my mother is way more devious than I've ever given her credit for. And I thought she was pretty devious before.

"The next time you try to hide something from me," Mother says dryly, "remember that I've known you and when you were lying your entire life. Also, I saw the maids doing some of her laundry."

So much for being stealthy. "But you said I shouldn't marry her."

Next to me, Lucy huffs in an indignant breath.

"I still don't think she's suitable." Mother doesn't even flinch as she says it. "But since it's not real, we can leave all this behind us. And we got rid of Archie."

My heart seems to crystallize, harden. I thought that admitting the lie would be the most difficult part, but I was wrong. It will be admitting that I love Grace since that's the most important part.

"We can't leave it behind." My voice is steady, almost stern. "Because I love her and I'm definitely going to marry her." When my mother opens her mouth, I cut her off. "There is no argument, no discussion. It's decided."

Shock and outrage roll through her expression. "You can't. I forbid it."

"I can. You trust me to run the company, lead the family. Trust me in this."

There's a moment where I see her wrestling with it, with everything that's changed between us. She's not in charge anymore, which is what she wanted, but it's also hard to give up. I understand. So I reach over, squeeze her hand. "It will all be fine. I promise."

There's a beat where she stares down at our joined hands, then she nods. Short and sharp, but she does it. "Now's not the time to discuss this." Her gaze meets mine. "But we will talk later. At length."

That's going to be unpleasant, but it's necessary. I did lie to her. "Of course."

"Um, what about Grace?" Lucy asks quietly. "Should we… go get her?"

Mother leans back, sighs. "You should explain all this from the beginning."

So I do, starting with Grace's job at Corvus, how she exposed their illegal programs, got fired for it, and couldn't get her visa approved with another company. And how Fuchs offered her her freedom for naming the person inside his company who's working against him.

"But she wouldn't do it?" Mother clearly doesn't understand why.

"It's complicated," I say. If Grace wants to tell the story of her great-uncle, she can. That's not my family secret to give. "But no, she couldn't. That's not who she is."

Lucy taps my arm excitedly. "Wait, what if *you* went to Fuchs? You give him the name, he gives Grace her visa, and she can come back."

I've been struggling with that same question as I tell the story—what to do about Fuchs?

"I can't go against Grace's wishes." I want to, but in the end she was right. "She doesn't owe Fuchs anything. I'm not giving him a damn thing, not even a response. Let him stew and do his own dirty work."

Grace and I don't need anything from him to start our life together. She can be done with him, finally and forever. And it will drive him stark raving mad to lose even that last small leverage he has against her.

"But you can't let him get away with it," Lucy says.

"We won't," Mother says simply. "We'll answer as a family. By stopping any of his business deals we can and souring his networking relationships."

I have to smile at her ruthlessness. Mother might have her reservations about Grace, but she's prepared to fight Fuchs for me. "Sounds perfect."

Lucy taps my arm again, this time with more force. "You still have to go find Grace though."

"I haven't forgotten." I look at the gala going on, at the people trying their best to listen in on our conversation. The gossip sites are going to explode tomorrow. "Look, can I leave you two to…?" I gesture around us, meaning our guests, the scene I've made, everything that isn't finding Grace and bringing her home.

"Of course." My mother says it with a touch of asperity, as if she can't believe I'd ever doubt her.

I kiss them both on the cheek, because they mean so much to me in their own, unique ways. "Thank you."

"Go." Lucy shoos me toward the exit. "Hurry up."

So I do, ready to take on ICE, Fuchs, and maybe, maybe even fly commercial if it will bring me back to Grace.

CHAPTER TWENTY-FOUR

A flight to China doesn't take as long as you might expect, even if you're awake the entire flight. It's only about twelve hours, and I spend all twelve dry-eyed and silent. I'm still in my gown, although one of the flight attendants gave me a blanket to wrap around my shoulders. "You can keep it," she whispered to me, no doubt sensing I was at rock bottom.

The ICE agents escorting me onto the plane probably gave that away.

The blanket is wrapped around my shoulders as I ride the subway to my parents' house. Several commuters have given me strange looks, but I don't think it's because of my dress and the blanket—I think it's because of the hollow look in my eyes.

I feel dead inside. Surely I must look that way too?

No one says anything to me though; everyone else is caught up in their own lives. I'm a curiosity, but in this massive city, another, better curiosity will turn up in a few minutes.

At my stop, I stumble out of the train and up the stairs, holding tight to my blanket. Beneath it I'm clutching my purse, which holds only my passport. I don't even have my national ID or money or anything. When my phone rang and

I yelled for Paul to save me, the agent managed to toss my phone out the window. I don't think it was an accident.

I'm returning home with literally nothing. The ICE agents said something about shipping my things to me, but I wasn't paying close attention.

January could probably pack my things up and ship them to me. Or Paul—

I force his image, even his very name, away from me. It hurts too much.

He's gotten what he wanted. His mother announced his new role as CEO of Tsai Holdings. She can't walk that back now without losing face.

That was the plan, the end game we were counting on. Paul assumes his role as head of the family and I go home. Perhaps it happened more quickly, more violently, than we were expecting, but this was supposed to happen.

I know Paul will hold up his end and that soon enough I'll have enough in my bank account to do whatever I like, including doing nothing at all for the rest of my life. And I held up my end; I pretended to love him so well that I ended up falling for him for real.

As I pass through the familiar streets, I keep my head high and my gaze on nothing. The thought of seeing a family friend, of having to smile and chat, is unbearable. If I don't look at anyone, I can pretend I see no one.

Too soon, my parents' apartment building appears. I key in the code, then walk all twelve flights up to our floor. My legs burn and my heart is racing, but I want the pain.

"Dad?" I call out in our dialect, the one only used in the village where my parents grew up. I suddenly feel like a child again.

"Zhenzhen?" He uses my Chinese name, the one he and my mother chose so carefully for me. Not the American name I picked for myself in school.

He and Mother always chose so carefully for me, and now

I've ruined it all. The tears run silently down my cheeks, my grief finally overflowing.

"I'm so sorry," I say. "They wanted me to expose someone, someone who was doing a good, brave thing, and I couldn't. I just couldn't."

My father embraces me, his arms so comforting, so familiar. I cry even harder. "Of course you couldn't do something wrong. Of course."

He says it over and over and over again until the words blur together into soothing nonsense. And he lets me keep crying on him.

Finally, when I'm as dried out as a desert and my head aches, I straighten up and wipe my eyes. "I'm sorry."

Dad hands me a tissue. "Don't be sorry. But… I don't understand. Why are you home?"

Oh. Oh boy, I have so much I have to tell him. I told my parents about losing my job, and I mentioned that I had a plan to get a new one, that everything would be taken care of… but I said nothing about Paul. Nothing about the deception I involved myself in.

Nothing about how I felt about him.

I can't talk about Paul, not now. Maybe someday, when it hurts less, I'll give my parents the entire story. But not today, not when I just got off the plane, the plane I was thrown onto.

"Arne Fuchs wanted me to betray someone to him," I say. "There's a person inside the company leaking information. He thinks I know who it is, and if I told him… he'd have my visa taken care of."

My father sighs as he sits back down. His knees aren't in good shape, and they creak as he does. "And the information was something bad?"

I try to think of how to explain the American surveillance state to a man who lives under one that is much, much worse. One that murdered his uncle.

"It was," I say. "The things they exposed needed to be revealed."

Dad nods. "Then you did the right thing."

It's as simple as that for him. His trust in me, in my judgment, is so weighty I almost cry again. I've disappointed him —I must have—coming back like this, but he's accepting the necessity of it because I've said so.

I sit cross-legged on the floor, my usual position. When I was younger, I could watch my father from here as he read the paper, did work, or spoke with guests. I still remember a particular evening when my father's uncle was here, the way he and my father sat together on the couch, talking about things I couldn't understand, my favorite doll tucked under the coffee table, a toy horse next to me.

My great-uncle is gone and so are my toys, but I still sit in this spot when I'm at home.

My skirt pools around me, the gold velvet stark against the plain beige rug of the living room. I should change, toss aside my blanket and put this dress far, far away from me, but if I do that, the last threads of fantasy will dissolve completely.

I pull the blanket tighter around my shoulders. "I tried so hard to stay." I sniffle again but catch myself before I start sobbing all over.

"I know." My father waves his hand as if shooing all my justifications away. "You've always done your best at everything you tried."

It doesn't feel that way though. There must have been something I could have done, some way that this didn't happen.

I only wish I'd told Paul… something. Maybe even that I love him, although if I see him again, that will make things awkward. He'd be too polite to say anything, but I would know.

He was going to tell me something after the gala though.

When our eyes met on stage, I felt it, the immensity of what was between us.

Or maybe that was the fantasy. The fear of being taken is seeping into all the memories of the gala, tainting them. Maybe what I think I remember wasn't there at all.

I put the heels of my palms into my eyes, my leftover makeup gritty on my skin. "I need a bath."

"And a meal," my father says. "But first some tea."

He brings me a cup, steaming and smelling of delicate jasmine. I take a deep breath of the steam and start to slump, the anxiety that's been holding me up for the past few hours finally dissolving.

"Thank you," I mumble. I could put my head on the coffee table and sleep right here. I did it as a child, and it looks so inviting now.

"Your mom should be home soon." Dad has sat back down on the couch in his usual spot. "She went out with some of her friends. She'll be so happy to see you."

She won't, although she'll hide it well. She'll be worried, scared, confused by my surprise arrival. Basically all the same emotions churning through me.

I take a sip of tea even though my stomach is very, very unhappy with me, because it would be rude not to. Too much traveling, too much trauma, too much everything in the past twenty-four hours.

My head droops, my eyes closing. I fight the exhaustion because I need to finish my tea, wait for my mother to come home, and somehow contact January and let her know that I'm fine. And Paul…

I'm asleep before I can finish the thought.

CHAPTER TWENTY-FIVE

Being home again is both agonizing and soothing at the same time.

To be in the familiar rhythms of life here, eating the foods I grew up with, speaking the dialect that was my first language, being among the people who know me best—it's the exact medicine I need for my broken heart.

But to see the cameras tracking everyone, going onto the internet hobbled by government censorship, being reminded of my great-uncle whenever I catch my father in a certain light, hurts my soul all over again.

In the end, I told my parents everything. About Corvus and Fuchs, and even about Paul. At least the fake engagement part. Not about falling in love with him.

They were shocked and confused and couldn't understand why I'd do such a thing—and why I'd lie to them about it—but I couldn't explain it in a way that made sense to them. Yes, I owed Paul for his help, but to fake an engagement? And lie to his entire family?

When they put it like that, shame sizzled through me. I should have told Paul no, that I wouldn't lie for him.

Except, if he asked me to do it all over again, I'd say yes. Love has turned me into a bad daughter.

In the end, my parents dropped it, probably assuming that my immigration troubles scrambled my mind for a time. They wouldn't be wrong.

So I've come home under a cloud of shame and disappointment. It's good to be back, but I also feel the weight of my parents' expectations in a more immediate way. They're happy to see me—but also very disappointed, even though they're trying hard not to show it.

Today hasn't been so bad though. After three days here, I've fallen back into the family life quite easily. The fish seller recognizes me now, and yesterday the butcher promised to save me a good chicken for the weekend. I'm walking back with my groceries, having found everything Mother will need for the dinner tonight. The neighborhood bustles and rushes around me, somewhere between a river and creek of humanity, exhilarating but not overwhelming.

An Instagram-ready group of girls passes me, holding up their phones as they chat into them. Behind them, a group of boys about their age watch with awe and longing, as if they can't believe such lively and beautiful creatures actually exist.

I call hello to the men sitting outside a noodle shop, cronies of my father's. He likes to sit with them and discuss the state of the world—nothing political, simply observations about young people and the New China.

From an electronic billboard overhead, Paul's face flashes out at me.

I yelp before I can catch myself. I know it's not him—he's ten feet tall for starters—but my heart jumps anyway. I duck under an awning, cutting off my line of sight. The billboard keeps flashing, and I have the terrible suspicion it's some gossip site talking about Paul's runaway fiancée and how he's waiting for the right girl to come along and heal his broken heart.

He hasn't contacted me, not that he would know how to find me. I never told him my parents' address, my phone was smashed by ICE, and I haven't dared to check my email addresses or social media accounts. Chinese customs wasn't too happy to hear I'd been deported back. Lying low is the wisest thing I can do.

I got a message out through a university friend to January, telling her I was fine and I'd contact her later, once things cool off. Her silence I was expecting—she's not going to come all the way here to check on me.

Paul… although there's nothing he can do that he hasn't already tried… I still keep hoping I'll see him. That somehow, someway, he'll appear, having magically solved all my visa problems.

Or better yet, he'll ask me to marry him. For real. It won't solve my visa problems, but it would heal my broken heart. Who needs a green card if you can have Paul?

I sigh, keeping my head down so I don't accidentally see the billboard. I haven't got a green card or Paul, so the question is pointless. I'm no princess waiting for her prince to appear with a magical shoe. Or a talking donkey or any other kind of enchanted item.

I suppose he could appear to give me the money he promised me, but that… I bite my lip, hard. The money would help, certainly, and I'm not so stupid as to turn it down, but when he gives it to me, our arrangement will officially be over. No more engagement, fake or otherwise. The fairy tale will be ended.

The billboard stays out of sight for the last few feet to the building door, the grocery bags suddenly heavy in my hands. Tomorrow, I decide, tomorrow I'll start looking for a job. No point sulking at home when I'm able-bodied and with such a good education. I'm no princess, so it's time I stopped acting like one.

When I reach the apartment door, I hesitate at the sound of voices on the other side. My parents didn't tell me we'd have guests. There's my father's voice, low and gravelly, weighted with all the years of his experience. And then another voice, a man's, bright and rich as polished jade.

My heart lurches. It can't be.

I set my shoulders, force my expression into calmness. It's not at all who I think it is, and I need to get ahold of myself.

With two fingers and a thumb, I wrestle open the knob. Instead of going into the living room and meeting our guest, I slip into the hallway that leads to the kitchen. I drop the bags on the counter, trying not to hear the voices coming from the other room.

It's not him; you're imagining things. Stop this.

My heart can't take it. I whirl around and march into the living room, determined to face whoever it is and convince my heart of its foolishness.

Only, my heart is right.

"Paul." It's all I can say as I stare at him, looking so crisp, so noble, as he sits with my father in my family home.

"Grace." The expression on his face is hopeful, agonized, open. Like he's in love and it terrifies him.

I close my eyes. No, no, no. I can't pretend that I'm seeing what's not there. "I don't want the money."

Ah, I could bite my tongue. Of course I need the money.

"Money?" Father says, lifting an eyebrow.

Paul turns, facing him. "I'm ashamed to admit that I bargained with your daughter, paying her for helping me in my deception."

My jaw sags open. Paul's told my father... everything? "What?"

He turns back to me. "I had to tell your father the truth. It was the only way I could ask him to let me marry you."

My knees are not working anymore, and the floor is rushing toward me. But Paul catches me, guiding me to a chair, kneeling before me and holding my hand. Just like a prince would.

"I don't understand."

My father rises, carefully looking past us. "I will go find your mother."

Before I can even think to call him back, he's gone.

I wet my lips, looking at Paul on his knees. "How are you here?"

He smiles. "I'm sorry I wasn't here sooner, but I had some business to attend to. Archie—who called ICE on you—had to be dealt with."

My skin goes cold. "Dealt with?"

Paul shrugs. "Cut out of the Hong Kong deal and all future family deals. He deserved more, but Mother reminded me he was family."

"Oh. I suppose it's always best to be merciful."

"I wasn't feeling merciful." His eyes are cold. "When I discovered what he'd done, I wanted to beat him to a pulp. But that was nothing compared to what I want to do to Arne Fuchs."

"I can't tell him who I think the mole is. I just can't."

"I know. Your father told me about your great-uncle too. I understand completely." His gaze softens as he squeezes my hand. "Fuchs won't bend. But we don't have to live in America. Give it a few years and we can apply again. They can't say no to my wife."

"But… the engagement was fake."

"It was. Until it wasn't. I think… I think it was the wrestling. There was this side of you I never expected, and it fit the side of me that I can't show to anyone else, and I saw… I saw that I could be myself with you. My entire self."

I sniff because it's so beautiful and I'm so happy to hear it. "But your mother. She'll be so angry."

"She was—is—but she likes you too. Mostly she's angry at me, not you."

"I'm not like Amelia. I don't know everyone, didn't go to the right schools, my accent isn't perfect—"

He kisses my wrist, openmouthed, and sends my mind

scrambling. "That doesn't matter. You're everything I need. Which I why I came to speak to your father today."

"What did he say?"

"He said I don't deserve you. That you are the daughter every father would wish for." Paul's smile goes wry. "And that if you said yes, he'd give his blessing."

I must be a princess because my father is an emperor straight out of a saga—wise and just and perfect. I blink away my tears because this is too happy a moment to start crying.

"I'm sorry I wasn't here sooner," Paul says again. "But now that I am, I have to tell you everything I couldn't after the gala."

Oh. I feel my heart melting a bit. He takes my face in his hands.

"I love you." He says it so simply I know it comes straight from his heart. "I love you, and I want to marry you. For real. There's no one else I want to walk through life with. So Grace, will you marry me?"

Okay, I tried not to cry, really, really hard, but this is too much. Tears are pouring down my cheeks, warm and salty, and I don't think I've ever felt *so much* in my entire life.

"Yes," I get out, my voice shaking. "Yes, I love you and I want to marry you too."

His smile is blinding. "We'll do it right away. No waiting, no engagement."

I have to laugh. "Yes, we've already done that. We're ready for the next step."

He kisses me again. I kiss him back, feeling like I've finally, finally come home.

"The next step is the rest of our lives," he whispers against my mouth. "And I can't wait."

CHAPTER TWENTY-SIX

I've already met Paul's mom, so I shouldn't be this nervous.

But this time I know she's going to be my mother-in-law for real. And that she's not exactly happy with me.

We're in one of the sitting rooms in the penthouse of a massive skyscraper Paul owns in Taipei. His mother is supposed to arrive for lunch at any moment. I already know I won't be able to eat a bite.

After spending a few days in Beijing with my parents—who absolutely fell in love with Paul and forgave him for everything—Paul whisked us off to Taipei. I already love it even if I haven't had much chance to explore it. The penthouse has a lovely view of Taipei 101, a massively tall skyscraper that makes me smile every time I see it.

"Lucy's coming in tomorrow," Paul says. He's sitting next to me on the low sofa, which is done in creamy white silk. It's also completely pristine, making me wonder how often people actually sit on it.

"Good." My voice is squeaky. "I can't wait to see her."

Paul takes my hand. "She's mad at me, not you. Don't be nervous."

"She might not be mad at me, but she still thinks I'm unworthy."

"You're my choice, which makes you most worthy. I'm the one who's unworthy."

I want to roll my eyes even if it is very sweet. He kept saying things like that to my parents, which they loved. *The* Paul Tsai wanted to be worthy of their daughter—how delightful!

My parents loved it, but his mother will not. "Don't say that to her," I warn. She doesn't want to hear that her son is unworthy of anything.

"I'll handle her," he says. "Really, she's mostly mad about the lying."

Great, because there's nothing I can do about any of that. I did lie, quite often and right to her face.

The door to the sitting room opens and I jump. Oh God, I'm not ready. I don't know if I'll ever be ready.

His mother sweeps in, dressed in a Chanel suit, carrying her usual handbag.

"Mother." Paul rises easily, kisses her on both cheeks. Clearly he's ready for this. "I've brought Grace."

I stand as she looks me over. Her mouth is flat, her expression unimpressed. This is even worse than when I met her the first time.

"I'm sorry," I say. Best to simply get it out of the way.

"You should be. Didn't your parents teach you lying is wrong? Especially to your elders?"

Paul steps between us. "We both knew it was wrong. But I asked Grace to do it and convinced her to go along. It was my idea."

I exhale and step around him. "I lied too. Paul may have suggested it, but the blame is mine as well."

His mother's chin lifts. "True. I'm glad to see you accept your blame in all this."

"I do." I set my shoulders. If I'm going to be Paul's wife, I need to stand up to his family when necessary, stand beside him. Even when we're standing against his mother.

"I know you want a wife who will support me, who will help me carry out my duties," Paul says gently. He gestures to a sofa, asking his mother to sit. She does, positioning herself so that she's pointing slightly away from him.

When we sit back down, Paul sits too close to me. We're touching, pressed against each other. It's… it's a bit impolite. But I'm so grateful for the physical acknowledgment of his support I don't move.

"I did." His mother flicks a glance at me that says she's not convinced I fit the bill. "You could have simply said that Amelia wouldn't suit you. You didn't need to lie."

Paul did say that to her, often. He told me about it.

"We hurt you and the family when we lied," I say. "And we are both deeply ashamed."

"You should be." But her posture has softened some.

Paul's hasn't though. "No matter how our engagement came about, Grace is my choice as a wife. I need a wife who will support all of me. Not only my work, not only my duties to the family. But…" He looks at me, his gaze intent. "But my heart as well."

Oh. I'm blinking too hard, too fast, but it's to keep from crying.

He faces his mother. "I'm going to run the company differently than you did. Because I am my own person. And Grace is the one woman in the world who fits me perfectly."

His mother swallows hard. It looks as if she's thinking of protesting more. Instead, she says, "I wish I'd had a partner. It's why I felt so strongly about your future wife."

Felt. My breath catches as that registers with me.

Paul inclines his head. "I know. But if you want me to run this company, lead this family, then I have to have Grace by my side to do it. There's no other way."

He doesn't look at me, but his hand finds mine, holds tight. I squeeze back.

His mother watches us. Her expression isn't yielding…

but it isn't as hard as it was. She says nothing for so long my pulse starts to sputter.

She's going to say no, that she'll never accept me. I don't know what we'll do then.

Finally she says to me, "Lucy hasn't stopped talking about you. Apparently if I do not agree to this marriage, both my children will renounce me."

I frown. She's not angry. Or harsh. It almost sounds like… a joke? Or something like it.

Paul is shaking his head. "Lucy's flair for the dramatic is rubbing off on you."

His mother sniffs dismissively. "No one could be as dramatic as she is. There isn't enough drama left in the world for that." Her gaze lands on me. "Both my children love you. And since I love my children…"

She doesn't finish that, not that I'm expecting her to. She's accepted me even if she can't exactly say that. Paul and I did lie, a big, long lie. We'll have to work to earn her forgiveness.

I respect her more for that.

"I love your children too." I glance at Paul. "One perhaps more than the other though."

A smile flickers at the corner of her mouth. "Has Paul shown you our island yet? There are many beautiful places here."

I let myself exhale completely. I've been invited in. "Not yet. We only just arrived."

The servants come in to tell us lunch is served. Paul rises, offering one arm to me and one to his mother. And we walk into the dining room together, his mother and me joined by Paul.

CHAPTER TWENTY-SEVEN

The Wedding of the Century sounds great and amazing and exactly the kind of party you want to go to... until the Wedding of the Century turns out to be your own wedding.

"I'm sorry. You expect me to do what?" My tone is respectful, but I want the wedding planner to understand that I'm not happy about that suggestion.

"Walk the mile to the church with your wedding party." The planner smiles as if I should be over the moon. "The press will be able to get so many pictures. And Grace will come in a carriage—"

"No." I lift my hands, ready to escape this interminable meeting. "I'm not parading myself right before my wedding."

"But the pictures..."

Next to me, Grace is hiding her smile behind her hand. "What Paul means, I think," she begins in a conciliatory tone, "is that it isn't quite our style. And yes, we know the latest British princess had it in her wedding, but we're looking for something more... traditional. Less exposed."

The wedding planner sighs. "Your mother wanted me to consider the PR aspects along with everything else."

Of course she did. She might have retired, but promoting the family interests remains my mother's main priority.

I just want to get married. To preserve the illusion of propriety, Grace is living in an apartment of her own here in Taipei, and I'm not supposed to be sleeping over. It's driving me crazy, along with the massive wedding plans I have to comment on. Colors, foods, even down to the individual flowers, require my rapt attention and approval it seems.

"You definitely have that aspect covered," Grace says. She glances at me. "Perhaps we can cover the rest later? Paul and I have another appointment."

We don't, but I keep my mouth shut as the planner leaves, letting Grace save me from any more of this.

Grace turns to me once she's gone. "You're the prince. The people want to see you."

I roll my eyes. Since the moment our engagement was announced—and we gave an exclusive interview detailing a highly polished and sanitized version of our love story—the press can't get enough of Grace. I'm yesterday's news as far as they're concerned.

"They'll get plenty of pictures," I say. "They don't need me parading down the street."

She sighs, but it's fake. "I was kind of excited by the carriage."

"You weren't." She's been handling the press attention pretty well, but I know it wears on her. Once we're married, it will settle down. Or else I'll have to call a bunch of tabloid editors into my office and explain things to them. "But I do have something that *will* excite you."

Sparks flare in her gaze, and I wish we were somewhere more private than a meeting room in the Tsai Holdings building. Anyone walking by the windows will see us.

"Are you sure I can't sneak into your bedroom tonight?" I mutter into her ear. "I'm dying."

She releases a regretful breath. "Me too. But your mother insisted. And think how amazing the wedding night will be."

"A week is too long." I check that no one's watching, then lean over and kiss her neck, making my way to her collarbone. Lord, but she smells so damn good.

"I know." She tilts her head back, gives me better access. "Wait. You said you had something for me and it wasn't this."

Reluctantly I raise my head because she's right, and I can't be caught making out with her in my own building. "Here." I find a file folder in a pile at my elbow, then pass it to her. "This is your wedding present."

She takes it with a frown. "I didn't buy you anything."

"You're my wedding present."

She shakes her head, but she's smiling too. And then her mouth opens as she reads through the contracts. "Is this…?" She looks up, disbelief in her eyes. "This can't be."

"It's real. It turns out you *can* buy an entire wrestling league if you want." I shift in my chair because it's not the usual wedding present—Lucy was appalled I wasn't buying diamonds—but this is so perfectly Grace I had to. "And it's all yours."

She hugs the folder to her chest. "I own a wrestling league. Me."

"You're going to make pro wrestling the biggest sport in China."

She laughs, then bites her lip. "Oh, what will your family think?"

I shrug. "They don't have to know. It's under the name of a holding company. And some things can be just for us."

She kisses me, deep enough to make me wish again we were somewhere else, or she was living with me, or we were married already. "I can't wait to see it."

"Oh, we're going tonight," I say. "There's a match starting in about two hours. And the jet is waiting."

"It's the most perfect present ever." The love and gratitude and happiness in her eyes makes me swallow hard.

"I'm glad you like it." I'm trying to catch my breath, but it's difficult when she's looking at me like that.

"I love it. And I love you." She smiles impishly. "Now let's go have some fun. Just for us."

ABOUT THE AUTHOR

Raleigh fell in love with billionaire romance as a teenager thanks to Harlequin Presents. She fell in love with San Francisco in her twenties thanks to how charming the city was. And she fell for a coding genius thanks to how charming *he* was.

Naturally, she had to put all of the things she loved into her romances.

You can find her online at www.raleighdavis.com.